Backed by You

A. Boss

PEAK EVEREST PUBLISHING

ISBN: 978-1-963564-08-2 (ebook)

ISBN: 978-1-963564-09-9 (paperback)

For everyone who discovered home isn't a place—it's a person.

"Home is wherever you are."

One.

Beau

"I said, I don't need it," I growl, attempting to maneuver around the flight attendant holding out the cane they forced me onto this damn plane with.

"But Mr. Montgomery, you—"

I stalk past the woman and down the aisle to the exit. My knee is stiff from the long flight, but it's manageable. I've been doing physical therapy nonstop for the last four months, during and after sessions. After two knee surgeries to repair the tendons and muscles and a full joint replacement—which a single stray bullet destroyed—I'm walking.

And like hell I'll be seen using a damn cane at thirty-three.

Deboarding the plane, I toss my military-grade backpack over my shoulder and head to baggage claim. It's surreal being back in Montana. *Home.*

After serving my country for the last fifteen years, I've been honorably discharged from the army. I wasn't ready to leave my brothers-in-arms behind, but life has a sick way of handing out cards, and this card...I'm going to have to play.

I'll be moving forward with my fallback plan of building and managing rental cabins in the popular ski resort mountains of Whitetail.

Between my parents and siblings, they've done a good job of managing my property and the two rentals while I've been away. But I'll be taking over everything. Hell, I'll need the distraction, because after getting shot in the fucking knee, my military career is over.

My jaw ticks as I come around the corner at the congested airport in Whitetail. My entire family is lined up beside the baggage claim with 'Welcome Home, Beau' signs. *Christ.* I mean, I get it. I haven't been home for over three years, but this isn't the homecoming I wanted. In fact, I didn't want one at all.

"There he is," my father booms.

"Beau," Ma shouts, rushing toward me.

I go through the motions of hugs and hellos. I plaster on a fake smile as best I can, but I'm willing to bet it looks more like a fucked-up grimace.

My four brothers, sister, nephew, my parents—everyone looks about the same as when I saw them last. Except now, there are two women I don't recognize with babies on their hips and wedding rings on their fingers—my apparent 'sisters-in-law' Ma mentioned on the phone a few months ago.

Duke introduces me to his wife, Maci, and their ten-month-old daughter, Olivia—who looks exactly like her mother, with deep red hair and green eyes, while Butch introduces me to his wife, Cassidy, and their nine-month-old son, Gage—a mini version of Butch with his mother's blue eyes.

Half my siblings seem to have started a family while I was away. Even my nephew Parker has sprouted like a weed since the last picture Lily sent me.

Meanwhile, I haven't felt the embrace of a woman in...a long time.

My chest tightens at the thought.

"How the hell are you, Beau?" Duke grins, giving me a burly hug.

I grunt.

"You look good, man," Rhett says. "How's the knee?"

"Fine," I say, reaching for my duffle on the rotating belt beside me.

Levi snatches the bag at the last second. "I've got it, man." He winks while hefting it over his shoulder. "No worries."

I grit my teeth. This is going to be more frustrating than I anticipated.

You could say I've gotten along with my siblings over the years. Mainly because I keep my mouth shut and watch the bullshit from the sidelines.

Not that our personalities match in the slightest from what I can remember. I'm a loner; they're all about family. I joined the military; they started businesses and stayed close to home. Hell, I'm the only one who's ever left the country.

"Is that all you have, sweetie?" Ma asks.

"Yeah."

"Well, let's hit it, kids." My father claps. "Your mother's got a roast waiting at home that's calling my name."

There's a collective bit of laughter amongst everyone. Except me. I was hoping to go straight to the cabin.

Duke slaps a hand on my shoulder. "You're riding with us, bro."

We head to his truck, and I take the front seat, while Maci and Olivia sit in the back. I stare out the window, taking in everything that's changed since the last time I was here.

"So, how was Washington, DC?" my brother asks, glancing between me and the road. "Ma said that's where they sent you after they got you back stateside."

"Best knee surgeon in the States is stationed there," I grumble.

He nods. "You, uh, feeling good? I mean, you look fuckin' great. Like you haven't taken a break from the gym or whatever the hell they had you doin' for recovery."

I've never been one to sit idly by when there's work to be done. Whether that's leading my squadron or pushing my body to heal—it's all the same to me.

I don't respond.

Maci clears her throat. "We talked to Callie and let her know that if she needs anything to give you a call. But, um, we don't have your new phone number to give her."

My brow furrows. "Who?"

"Callie Ryan," Duke says, like I'm supposed to know who that is. "She's your tenant. She moved into the one-bedroom cabin, been renting it for four months."

"Almost five," Maci corrects.

Right. She's the one staying in *my* cabin. The one my mother was supposed to make sure was vacant for me when I got home. But lines got crossed, and it was already rented out before I made it known I wanted it for myself. "Got it."

"Maci and I, we've sort of taken over all the scheduling for the other cabin," he tells me. "Maci set you up a sweet website and everything. It's been blowing up with bookings."

She leans forward from the back with a kind smile. "I made sure it was free for you this weekend, though. Well, the next three nights at least. It's kind of booked after that..."

I scowl. *Fuck.*

"Ma thinks you're going to want to stay at the house, but I figured we'd offer up our spare bedroom before she hounded you," Duke says.

"Thanks, but I'll figure something out."

Duke raises a brow. "You sure, Beau? I mean, Butch's got a spare room, too. Rhett and Levi got a pullout couch. Wherever you want. Lily's working on moving out of Ma's finally, so if you want to stay there, I doubt it'd be a big deal."

I huff. The idea of staying with any of my family sounds more fucking miserable than sleeping in the deserts of Iraq with active gunfire.

I don't need this kind of back-and-forth right out the gate.

"Um, there are breaks between bookings," Maci says quietly. "Usually so Julie can clean between renters, but if you're looking for somewhere to stay, I'm sure you can in between. If you don't mind moving around to get a little privacy."

I nod. *That*, I can deal with.

Changing the subject, I ask, "Did you take a look at that truck I sent you? Is it worth the money for what I'm planning on doing with it?"

Duke sighs, rubbing the back of his neck. "Yeah, it's a good truck. I let Steve at the dealership know you were flying in today. Said he'd hold it for you to have a look for yourself."

"Good."

"You're not gonna take a fuckin' break to save your life, are you?" my brother mutters.

Not if I have anything to say about it.

"Duke, I've been sitting on my ass for the last five months. Working through recovery, physical therapy, and dealing with getting discharged. I don't need a fuckin' break, all right? What I do need is for everyone to get off my ass when I just got back in town."

He shakes his head, turning down the driveway to my parents' place.

Three years since I've set foot in Montana, since I've been home… Three long, lonely years. And all I want is to be left alone.

I stare up the road toward my property, itching to get over there and start blocking off measurements for the next cabin. The very idea of manual labor has my blood heating. *I need that*, I realize. Sweat on my brow, the familiar ache in my muscles from a hard day's work, the peace that kind of solitude brings me.

My family may think thrusting me into some bonding dinner party is what I need right now, but it's the last thing I want.

And it sure as shit ain't the kind of lonely I need fixing.

After dinner—and countless pictures with *everyone*—I try to get away and head to the cabin, but I'm thrown into more talking about this 'double wedding' happening in less than two months for Butch, Duke, and their women.

Which sounds like a waste to me, given they're already married, but what the hell do I know? All I want is to get to the cabin, shower, and go to bed so I can start fresh in the morning with my list of projects.

I stand from my father's favorite recliner in the living room—he wasn't fooling anyone by insisting I sit here. I've been breathing Montana air for less than six hours and I've had enough coddling for a lifetime. "Thanks for dinner, Ma, but I think I'm going to head out. I'm pretty beat."

"You can take my truck tonight, Beau," my father says, tossing me his truck keys.

I catch them. "Thanks." I lift my chin to Butch, the logger of the family. "I'll give you a shout when I get the land blocked out and we'll get those trees hauled away."

He eyes me, judging, but keeps his thoughts to himself. "Sounds good."

Rhett raises his beer in my direction. "I'll put the lumber order in as soon as you get the building specs, brother. We've got you."

After a quick goodbye, I head to the truck and toward the cabin. It's a short ride, a mile curve up the road, but that's about the distance between my family on this mountainside.

I park in front of the two-bedroom rental and breathe a heavy sigh as I take in the familiar sight. Well, it might as well be *un*familiar with how many damn potted and hanging flowers are all over the place. *Did my mother do this?*

I've never been one for flowers.

The majority seem to be centered around the single-bedroom cabin. The front porch, along the cabin side, the stone walkway, the driveway—they're fucking *everywhere*.

I get out, staring at the outdoor rustic, black lantern light mounted beside the front door—idly noting it doesn't match the one on the other cabin. It crosses my mind that I should introduce myself, but I decide against it.

I'm already irritated enough this evening.

I walk up the steps of the two-bedroom cabin where I'll be crashing for the next three nights, the soreness in my knee reminding me to do my nightly stretches.

When I unlock the door, a car pulls in behind me. I turn as a baby-blue Jeep Wrangler with the top down and the doors off, whips in beside my father's truck.

My brow furrows as the wild woman driving throws it in park, carelessly leaving the Jeep angled at forty-five degrees and the wheels turned to the right. Not even *close* to properly straight. Doesn't she know that leaving a car parked in such a state is bad for the drive shaft *and* alignment?

My irrational irritation soon fades when a goddess hops down from the driver's seat.

Light grey sweatpants, a white tank top, and pink flip-flops. Sunkissed tan skin, hourglass curves, honey-blonde hair in loose curls that stop with a bounce just above her shoulders.

I'm awestruck.

And a fuckin' moron.

She reaches into the backseat of her car, her sweats stretching taut over her plump ass and making my cock thicken. Thighs, ass, hips, the dip of her waist, her ample chest—no bra and pert nipples. Even the slightest details have me captivated…from the peppered freckles along her shoulder blades to the small rose tattoo on her exposed ankle.

This can't be my tenant.

A loud, aggressive bark snaps me back to reality.

A giant-ass German Shepherd leaps down from the passenger seat. This dog is easily three times the size of any German Shepherd I've ever seen.

He stands behind the woman…protectively.

Honey-blonde locks whip in surprise over a gorgeous face free of makeup and… *Fuck.* Her full lips part, hazel doe eyes wide with thick lashes that grab at the heart strings I didn't know I had.

Everything about her looks like *honey*. Eyes, hair, skin.

She's the most beautiful woman I've ever seen.

But when she scurries to grab her wallet and a plastic to-go bag, my brow furrows as the dog stays beside her, pressing his body against her thigh while watching *me*. And as they reach her cabin door, I realize this is, in fact, my tenant—Callie Ryan—*with* a dog.

I thought I made it clear to Duke when I said, *"No pets allowed."*

No exceptions.

Two.

Callie

IF I HAD KNOWN big men who stare for far longer than necessary were the kind of people Duke and Maci, my landlords, rent out to, I would've opted for elsewhere.

I lock eyes with the towering man standing on the front porch steps of the larger vacation rental that neighbors my quaint little log cabin. I've been renting here on the outskirts of a small town in Montana known as Whitetail for nearly five months now, and this is the first time a tourist has given me the creeps.

I take in the unwelcome sight of my temporary neighbor and note just how intimidating he really is. He barely clears the sloped roof over the front porch, and at my shorter five-foot-five, he has to be over six-and-a-half feet tall. Broad and burly like an ox from his thick, vein-lined forearms. His biceps, covered by his beige T-shirt, have the fabric stretched to the point that if he tries to flex, it'll tear right off him like one of those *Thunder from Down Under* pretty boys.

His T-shirt is tucked into a pair of camo pants and there are two military-like bags set at his feet clad in combat boots. His dark hair is buzzed on the sides, leaving it a bit longer on the top. A faint dusting of a five o'clock shadow grows on a strong jaw that's locked tight as his intense gaze meets mine.

He's handsome...in an angry sort of way that only puts me on high alert.

Hulk, my service dog, presses his sturdy frame against the side of my thigh, a low growl building in his chest, alerting me of my racing pulse and the presence of this unexpected visitor.

Hulk is not only a PTSD certified service dog, he's also a fully trained police attack dog. I *know* what he's capable of. I've had him since he was a chunky puppy at six months old. My father, Matthew Ryan, is an officer who trains K9 units. Specifically, German Shepherds and their handlers. I grew up watching him train them.

Unfortunately, as Hulk grew and grew, he was deemed *too* big to be a police dog, regardless of the fact he passed the course with flying colors. If there was ever a scenario where he needed to be carried by his handler... Well, it'd be a little tough.

At a whopping one hundred and twenty pounds of muscle, forty inches to the withers, and a reach of over six feet standing on his hind legs, he's a purebred German Shepherd the size of a Great Dane. A true anomaly among his litter.

We formed a bond early on that even my father could tell was unbreakable. And after one too many stalkers, crazed fans, and being robbed at a gas station four years ago, Hulk hasn't left my side since. He watches my back and all my surroundings. Whenever there's a threat, he signals me and keeps me grounded and calm.

When I need him the most, he's always there for me.

He's my best friend.

My big baby.

I grab my wallet, keys, and the dinner we picked up from one of the local pizzerias before heading toward the cabin. Hulk stays at my side as we step onto my cute front porch filled with blooming flowers on this late spring evening.

The man grunts loudly.

I glance at him still watching me as I unlock the door. I try to get a feel if he's a threat or not, and I absently wonder if I should call Maci to find out how long this guy is staying for.

Should I get a hotel room until he's gone? I don't need the added anxiety.

"No dogs," he says, his voice a deep, husky growl that doesn't quite have the Western twang most people have around here.

My brow furrows. "Excuse me?"

"No. Dogs," he repeats, like that's supposed to explain his ignorant statement any further.

I roll my eyes and turn to the front door. When I push inside, I get the urge to say something. Normally I keep to myself with any of the obnoxious vacation renters I've come across since moving in. I never *want* to cause any problems, but... This guy is already pushing my buttons with his leering, and now his comment about Hulk, even though he's not wearing his service vest at the moment.

"How about you mind your own business," I say, shooting him a heated glare and striding inside with Hulk. I close and lock the door behind me, being sure to slide the extra deadbolt and slip-chain lock I installed.

The cabin is a typical one-bedroom, one-bathroom log cabin with a covered porch off the back that matches the one on the front. Rustic, quaint, wholesome. My perfect mountainside hideaway.

I walk to the left where the small kitchen-dining area sits with a sliding glass door that leads to the back. The four-seater dining table feeds into the living space where I've updated the original furnishings: a brown leather couch, end tables, a matching coffee table across from the stone fireplace, and a make-shift office with a desk beside the window for more natural light.

To the right is the bedroom where I've got a pillow-top, king-sized bed, a cluttered closet, a dresser, and a TV mounted on the wall. Through the bedroom, the bathroom is attached. A simple, standing glass shower, toilet, and sink set up—where I added new shelving for proper storage.

Even with all my updates and homey touches, I've kept some of the bear and deer décor that decorated the cabin when I first moved in.

Call it *Montana Inspiration*, if you will.

You could say I've been channeling that middle-of-nowhere atmosphere just by reading my latest screenplay. Because it's what I do, I'm a screenwriter—or as my loving and *supportive* father used to call it, "*Wasting my time.*"

Key words being: used to.

At the prime age of twenty-eight, I've sold over fifteen screenplays in the horror movie genre, with two completed films in a trilogy, and the third releasing in just six short weeks.

When you're young, well off financially, and sort of famous, one can gain a lot of unwanted attention from seemingly kind people with ulterior motives.

Hulk has needed to put his multitude of training to good use against a few close encounters. I don't know what it is about me, but people seem to think a petite blonde woman who writes about serial killers is someone they can try to take advantage of.

It's why I came here, to a small town barely on the map if it wasn't for the rising popularity of Winton's Ski Resort. Thanks to one of my best girlfriends back in LA, Shea Winton, I found this mountain paradise.

I set the to-go bag on the counter and grab a treat for Hulk. I give it to him with a kiss on the nose. "Good alerting, big boy," I coo.

I shuffle to the fridge to pull out the chicken breast I mix in Hulk's high-end, premium dog food for his dinner. He gets two of these fancy meals a day, with a variation between chicken, steak, and ground beef. I spare no expense to take the best care of him. He does the same for me.

Prepping his dinner, I hit play on the Bluetooth speakers I had installed throughout the cabin. The music bumps, and I sway my hips as I get to cooking with Hulk waiting patiently beside me.

It's not another five minutes later when I have the chicken in the frying pan on a low simmer that someone pounds on my door. Hulk's ears perk on high alert. He watches the door, but remains at my side.

I bet it's that asshole renter come to complain about my music *and* dog.

I snatch my phone off the table and lower the music. I hit dial on Maci's number and hold the phone to my ear as I walk to the front door with Hulk. I unlock the two deadbolts and chain, then finally the knob itself. I open the door to reveal the same towering brute from before.

"*Pass auf,*" I say, the German command for Hulk to guard the door from allowing anyone or anything from entering.

Hulk takes point at the door, positioning himself between me and the man glowering in my direction. He looks between Hulk and me, his scowl deepening.

"Hello?" Maci finally answers.

"Hey, Maci. It's Callie," I say, glaring at the obnoxious renter. "I've got some asshole over here banging on my door. He has two seconds to get off my porch before Hulk gets a taste of soldier boy."

The man at my door raises a stern brow, standing a little taller as he crosses his large arms over his insanely broad chest. Jeez. With that pose, he'd have to turn to the side just to walk in my front door.

"Oh—Oh my god," Maci whispers before frantically speaking to someone on the other end. "No, no, Callie. It's fine. Duke and I will be there in just a minute. Please, don't—"

"No pets allowed inside the cabins," the jerk grinds out through clenched teeth. "Chain up your dog outside, or you're both gone."

I bristle at his tone. "Who the hell are *you* to tell me where *my* dog is allowed?"

"And turn down that fuckin' music," he bites out, ignoring my question.

"Absolutely, *not*," I snap. "This is *my* house. I live here. Not you. You're just some dickhead who'll be gone by the end of the week."

"Callie, no, that's—" Maci tries to say.

"I want all these flowers gone. It's not a goddamn greenhouse out here," he demands. "And what the fuck is that raised block out back? What are you growing in there? Marijuana?"

I wish.

Hulk takes a menacing step forward with a rumbling growl in warning.

"*Blieb*," I command him to stay, and he returns to his original position.

The man snarls, glaring at Hulk, then me. "Like I said, no dogs."

"He's a service dog," I finally say. "He has every right to be anywhere and everywhere I am. Now get off my porch before I call the police."

The towering man's brow furrows, but before he can say anything, Duke's truck pulls in the driveway behind my car. Maci gapes at me from the front seat as she hangs up the phone.

"What kind of service dog?" Big Jerk asks.

"None of your damn business, that's what kind," I sass with a heated glare.

Duke jumps out of his truck and jogs over. "Beau! Christ, man. You really know how to make a first impression."

Beau?

Wait...

My mind trails back to the conversation I had with Maci roughly a week ago when she told me Duke's brother, Beau, is the one who owns the cabin I'm renting. This whole time I've been leasing from them on his behalf while he's been away. But when she said 'away,' she didn't elaborate, just that he'd be back soon and taking over rent and maintenance.

Is *this* my new landlord?

Big Jerk—or *Beau*—gestures to me while speaking to his brother. "I told you, no fucking pets."

Duke nods. "Yeah, I know, but Hulk's a service dog. You can't deny a tenant when you're listing as no pets if the animal is certified."

I sigh heavily. This is going to be a while. I hustle to the kitchen to turn off the stove, where the chicken is now overcooked.

Hulk barks in warning, and I turn to Beau watching my every move. "Where's his certification? And shouldn't he be wearing a vest of some kind?"

"He doesn't need to wear it when they're at home, man." Duke huffs, peeking his head in. "I'm sorry, Callie, but could you grab the papers to show him?"

I nod, thumbing through my wallet and removing Hulk's certification card, marking him as a PTSD service dog. I hand it to *Duke* to show his giant dick of a brother who should've *kindly* told me who he was, instead of coming at me like a bull seeing red.

Duke hands it off, and I watch Beau look it over. I take a deep breath, willing myself to answer any asinine questions he may have. They're always the same: How old is he? Where did he go to doggy service school?

What caused you to need a service dog?

His dark eyes peer at me a moment later. He doesn't say a word as he simply hands me the card.

I take it, tucking it in the waistband of my sweats. "He wears his service vest in public," I tell him. "I don't leave it on him at home. His collar also states he's a service dog as well, but it can get hidden by his fur."

Duke grins. "See? It's all good."

Beau grunts in response.

I bite my lip, gazing down at my buddy still on guard. "*Steh platz*," I whisper, letting him know he can stand down. Hulk takes a step back beside me, sitting at my feet with his side pressed against my leg and a watchful eye on Beau *and* Duke.

Hulk's been around Duke enough to know he's not a threat. If anything, he gets excited when he sees Duke's truck because he usually has Maci with him. And wherever Maci is, so is their baby girl, Olivia. And Hulk *loves* babies.

Beau's brow furrows even deeper. "Why would a service dog know German commands?"

I cross my arms over my chest in challenge. Because *that* is something I will *not* be sharing with anyone. Let alone this guy.

Duke slaps a sturdy hand on his brother's shoulder. "I think what my brother is trying to say is, he's sorry for the confusion."

I highly doubt that's what he's trying to say.

I tip my head to really look at this mountain of a man. I force a smile, extending my hand to him. "Callie Ryan," I say. "Your tenant."

Beau stares down his nose at me, his dark gaze scanning my face. He takes my hand in his rough, calloused hold. His large palm swallows mine as he gives it a shake with a firm, yet gentle grip.

"Beau Montgomery," he says before releasing my hand and turning to Duke. "Did you give her permission for all the flowers and the raised box in the back?"

Seriously? Just when I thought we were getting somewhere...

Duke opens his mouth to respond, but I chime in, "It's a vegetable garden. I'm going to plant some tomatoes, cucumbers, beans, a few bell pepper plants."

Beau's heated expression only burns hotter. "That doesn't answer my question. Did you or did you not get permission to dig up the yard?"

I scrunch my nose. "Dig up the yard? I didn't dig up anything. It's a raised garden box, I put soil on top, you know, inside of it."

"So, no. You didn't get permission," he grumbles.

"I don't need anyone's permission to put a raised garden in my backyard," I say, having to add, "Especially yours, *buddy*."

Beau's jaw tightens.

"I told her she could." Duke flat-out lies on my behalf. "The garden, the flowers, the tree. All of it I said was fine by you."

Beau snaps his head to his brother. "Tree? What tree?"

I wave a hand over my shoulder. "The baby elm tree beside the raised garden. I planted it. The space seemed a little...empty."

Beau shakes his head with an angry growl. He turns on his heel and stomps off my porch like some prissy diva who didn't get their way. "Keep your fuckin' music down, clean up after that dog, and move your Jeep into a real damn spot," he hollers.

"Whatever you say...Sergeant Dickhead," I mutter, earning a low chuckle from Duke. Beau hears me and whips that scowl over his shoulder in my direction.

I sigh. This isn't the kind of bickering first impression I wanted. And certainly not from a renter to a landlord. I like living here, it's treated me well so far, and I want to stay. Not get evicted.

"Sorry about him," Duke says. "He flew in earlier today, had a long day catching up with everyone. He's probably just tired."

I snort. "So, I guess now would be a bad time to tell him the oven stopped working."

Duke chuckles. "Yeah, might want to save that one." He pulls out his phone. "I can let him know, but if you want to take down his number, I'll give it to you now."

I nod, putting Beau's number in my phone. I fight the urge to label it as 'Sergeant Dickhead' since that seems to suit him oh-so-well. I say a quick thank you and goodbye to Duke, and I give Hulk another treat before I return to prepping his dinner.

I also turn my music back on...a *little* bit quieter.

After dinner, I clean up, take a shower, and tug on a pair of pajama shorts and an oversized hoodie. I pour myself a glass of wine and take Hulk out back. The sun sets over the picturesque mountain view, and I move toward the stone fire pit off the back porch.

I drag over a lawn chair while Hulk wanders to the tree line where he's allowed to take care of his business—it makes it easier for me to find his dumps and toss them into the surrounding forest. I pick a few pieces from the dwindling wood pile and take them to the fire pit.

That's when I see him.

Beau—*Dickhead*—Montgomery.

Standing on the back porch of his cabin, he eyes me like a disgruntled boss who doesn't approve of the work I'm doing. He's shirtless now, leaving it *all* on display—rather proudly, I might add. A pair of basketball shorts hanging dangerously low on his hips. His muscles are thick, chiseled like a sculpture with dark hair patched over his chest and leading...*down*. Strong thighs, bulky calves.

My gaze lands on a black sleeve of some kind covering the majority of his left leg with a brace around his knee. Huh. *Is that why he's home? Did he get hurt?*

I silently wonder what could hurt a man like Beau.

Trying to brush off the wound-up feeling brewing at his presence, I position the few pieces of wood in a teepee. I take the piece of junk mail and the lighter from my hoodie pocket and work on starting the fire.

Hulk trots over, sitting stoically beside me, watching my back like always. I'm sure he's keeping an eye on our nosey neighbor. Or landlord, I suppose. I'd like to think he's not a threat to me...

You don't know it for a fact.

The crackle of the fire has me taking my seat. My chair is angled so I can look out over the setting sun that's filling the evening sky with stunning waves of natural hues.

I scratch behind Hulk's ears—his favorite spot—and enjoy the low-burning fire as the slow cover of night falls upon us. Bravely, I steal a glance toward Beau who's still standing on his porch. It's a toss-up whether he originally came out here to spy on me, or if he, too, came out to watch the sunset. Because the second the sun is gone, he retreats into his cabin.

For a split second, I feel a twinge of guilt for not inviting him to sit with me. Then I remember his rude, unsolicited commentary regarding my flowers, garden, tree—my dog.

Let's hope he doesn't give me a hard time when I pick up the porch swing I had custom-made tomorrow.

He shouldn't mind, right?

Three.

Beau

I'M UP AND MOVING before dawn. I've slept better propped against fucking boulders than I did last night. I had this moronic sense that I acted like a real prick yesterday, and now I can't seem to get *her* out of my head.

Callie Ryan.

For a gorgeous woman with a body that could make any grown man insane, she's sure got a mouth to match. I put her on the defensive during our first encounter, but I've got questions—questions that are causing my curiosity to spike beyond belief.

Starting with why her dog, Hulk, follows German commands but is a certified PTSD service dog? Why does she need a service dog in the first place? Is he trained for another type of protection?

It sure as hell seemed that way based on how he was behaving toward her *against* me.

Her comment about Hulk getting a taste of my ass showed me just how serious she was about not taking any shit from me. Problem with that is, she has to. This is my property, my cabin. What I say goes. Whether she likes it or not.

So, I walk the property line beside her cabin, measuring the next two additional cabin sites that'll be built beside hers. I mark the trees that need removing with spray paint and tape off the sections accordingly. And since the dealership doesn't open for another hour, I start cutting down brush.

The rip of the chainsaw echoes through the tree line, and a sick thrill spikes my pulse when a feminine shout reaches my ears. I suppress a grin and glance over my shoulder to see her standing on the front porch of the cabin. She's wearing those damnable pajama shorts from last night where her ass was hanging out.

My hands twitch at the passing image of running my hands over the perfect honey-glow of her bare shoulders, midriff, and tan legs.

I swallow hard.

Fuckin' hell.

She's yelling at me, but I can't hear it over the roar of the chainsaw. I wait a beat, mainly just to piss her off, then shutdown the machine in hand.

"—It's 7:16 AM!" Her voice is a sexy, angry rasp with that hint of an accent I haven't quite placed yet.

She's got a 'city girl' aura around the way she speaks.

I grunt. "And?"

She throws her hands in the air. "It's too early to be doing whatever the hell it is you're doing. It's Saturday."

I raise a brow. "It's my property. I can do whatever I want, whenever I want."

She glares at me. "I live here."

"I'm well aware of that." I shoot a pointed look at her Jeep she never repositioned like I told her to.

"I—I'll file a noise complaint," she says, and I cock a half grin.

I tip my chin to her. "Go ahead, I'm listening."

She narrows her eyes at me. "To the police."

"Like I said, this is my property. I'm your landlord, you're my tenant. If you're going to file any noise complaints, it'd be to me." I fight to contain the shit eatin' grin itching to spread across my face at her sass.

She crosses her arms over her ample chest as she huffs her frustration. And just when I think she's going to give me an earful, she spins on her heel, storming into the cabin with a slam of the door.

I wonder if she envisioned it hitting me in the face, given the force she put behind that.

I release my burning grin and chuckle as I start the chainsaw and get to work.

My morning peace is then interrupted by her blaring music. The same shit she played last night. And I *swear* she didn't turn it down one damn bit after I told her to. Now...she's got it cranked to the max.

I shake my head, doing my damnedest to brush off the building irritation this woman is causing. I kill the rumble of the chainsaw and begin dragging the cut brush to the bed of my father's truck for his burn pile.

The blaring music abruptly stops, and I glance up to see Callie walking out with Hulk at her side. He's wearing a black and royal blue vest with 'service dog' written on either side. There are a slew of patches on the vest: Do Not Touch. Working Dog. Certified Service Animal. And an insignia to show his credentials.

Her high-waisted leggings, off the shoulder peach crop top, and sneakers have my cock weeping. Her honey hair bounces in loose curls, a light coat of makeup that suits her fuckin' beautifully.

It's infuriating the reaction my body has to the very sight of her.

She walks to her Jeep, and Hulk jumps in the front seat. She leans in to hook him into some kind of harness attached to the seatbelt. Gorgeous hazel eyes catch my stare for a moment, and my throat bobs uncomfortably when she sends me a stunning smile.

A smile so fucking breathtaking I don't know what to do with myself.

It's not meant for you, idiot.

I scowl.

She hops in the driver's seat and backs out before heading toward town—leaving me a puddle in the brush with a hardening cock.

I finish roughly half the brush removal before the truck is full. After a quick shower and change of clothes, I meet up with my father to head to the dealership.

I go through the motions of buying myself a newer four-door, extended-cab, charcoal grey pick-up. They let me know it'll be ready to be picked up tomorrow.

We get lunch at the diner, and I chat with Butch about the deep-rooted trees I need gone. I rattled off basic specs to Rhett on my lumber order to get that underway.

I'm feeling productive as hell until every-damn-one of them feels the need to make multiple comments on me needing to 'relax' or 'take a break.'

"Is all this labor good for your knee?"

To them—no, it's not good.

To me—I work through the pain. I always have. I do my physical therapy, but I don't lie to myself. At the end of the day, I'm sore. I'm hurting here and there depending on how I'm moving, but it's nothing I can't handle.

I manage just fine.

I pull in beside Callie's Jeep, parked even wilder than before. She has it backed in with the tailgate open like she was unloading something.

That's when I see her.

She's reaching up high under the sloped roof of the front porch with a drill in hand. She's recklessly standing on a chair of all things. On her damn tippy toes to do whatever the fuck it is she's doing.

I growl under my breath as I get out.

Hulk catches sight of me first, giving a loud, aggressive bark my way, alerting his owner of my presence. "Oh, hey," Callie says, peering under her arm at me.

As I approach, I stare at a set of chains sitting on top of a wooden bench swing that wasn't here this morning. "What are you doing?"

Bracing herself, she steps down from the chair. "I got a porch swing," she announces proudly. She smiles, pointing to the handcrafted swing. "Isn't it beautiful? I had it custom-made by this guy in town. It came out way better than I expected."

"Did Duke give you authorization to be drilling holes in the roof?"

Her face scrunches as if she's tasted something sour. "What is it with you and this *authorization* and *did you get permission*? It's a swing, Beau. A harmless, pretty porch swing. And in order to hang it properly, I need to drill holes for the hooks into the roof. Is that okay?"

She says it so sweetly, I almost give in. *Almost.*

"No," I deadpan.

"What do you mean, no?"

"No. It's not okay." I gesture to the drill in her hand. "Defacing private property is a criminal offense."

She raises a brow as she peers between the drill and me. "Are you going to file charges against me for two holes drilled in a porch roof for the purpose of hanging a porch swing?"

Why does that sound like a challenge?

"Return the swing," I say before turning to take my leave. However, her unexpected laughter has me stopping dead in my tracks.

She giggles. "No."

I face her. "You're not hanging that damn swing. And you better start looking into ways to patch those fuckin' holes, or I *will* press charges."

Callie smiles brightly, setting down the drill before reaching for the arm of the swing. She bends to pick it up and my jaw ticks, knowing it's real wood and likely heavy as hell.

"Are you going to help me?" she asks sweetly, gazing up at me through fluttering lashes.

I let out a heavy, aggravated sigh. "Callie."

"Beau," she mocks, smiling as she continues to drag the swing up the steps.

I shake my head and force myself to walk away. I won't be enabling her stubborn behavior.

It's just a porch swing. It's not. If I help her, it defeats the entire point I'm trying to make, that she can't do whatever the hell she wants like she owns the place.

She's a renter. *Not* an owner.

Stalking to my cabin, I glance back at her watching me with surprised eyes. Letting her do it by herself isn't the chivalrous thing to do, but it sure as fuck is proving my point. So, standing here with my arms crossed, leaning against the porch post, I watch her glare at me.

She hauls the swing into position, chains it up through the necessary hooks. Then moves her unstable chair to where she can lift the chain to the hooks she drilled into the goddamn roof.

My body fights me to go over there, seeing her struggling to get the chain on the hook where she wants it. This stubborn woman is going to be the death of me.

But before I can go over there and either help or give her another piece of my mind on her installing this fucking swing without my say, the signature *'Blip Blip'* of a police car sounds, pulling into the driveway.

Callie's gaze snaps to the Whitetail Deputy Sheriff car pulling in front of her Jeep. And out steps Justin White, the apparent deputy, and prick I went to high school with.

Roughly standing at six-foot, clean shaven, short dirty blond, slicked-back hair, wearing the traditional tan cargo pants and brown uniformed, short-sleeve shirt with all his gear strapped on him. The obnoxious smile he's beaming in Callie's direction has my jaw clenching and my eye twitching.

Callie gets down from the chair at the same time Justin speaks with that same irritating grin in his voice, "What you got goin' on there, Miss Ryan?"

I catch her glance at me, probably wondering if I called the cops on her, when I never truly would. But the threat still holds merit, depending on how this little interaction goes.

Justin approaches her front porch, and Hulk is sure to create his own barrier beside Callie. One I'm rather grateful for at the moment because I don't like how this fucker is eyeing her up. "You can call me Callie, Justin." She sighs. "I'm just hanging up my new porch swing."

Justin nods, looking at the swing before scanning the area, and that's when his eyes catch mine. "No shit. Beau Montgomery." He smirks. "How the hell are you, man? I heard what happened. Glad to see you made it outta there alive."

I grunt, not wanting to share any friendly banter with this fuckhead.

Callie looks at me curiously, likely wondering what he's referring to, but it wouldn't surprise me if she didn't already know. Turning her attention to Justin, she asks, "What, um, did you need, Justin?"

He grins. "Just checking in, make sure you're doin' well."

"He called you again, didn't he?"

"Officer Ryan did put in a wellness check," he says, resting his hands on his utility belt, like he's someone even remotely important. "Said you haven't been answering any of his calls."

She huffs in annoyance. "I missed *one* call. I was in the middle of a project; he knows I always get back to him when I can."

Justin nods. "Yeah, I figured as much. But you know how it goes, get the call, gotta check in." He points to the porch swing. "Need any help hanging that up?"

I move. Pushing off the post, I stalk my way over, grumbling several curses under my breath as I catch Callie's eye and the stunning smile that follows. She gestures my way. "Thank you, but Beau was just coming over to help me."

Justin raises a brow when I walk past him and onto Callie's porch to hang this goddamn swing, because like hell I'm watching *Deputy Justin* help her.

"You sure, Beau? I'd hate to see you mess your knee up. After all those surgeries it took to put you back together."

I snarl, ignoring him. I hoist up the chain and swing, getting it hooked, hung, and level within seconds. Callie beams, craning her delicate neck up to look at me. "Thank you."

Justin clears his throat loudly. "Well, I'd better get going. It was good seeing you, Callie. Tell your father I said hello when you get a chance to call him back." He winks with a chuckle, retreating on his heel to his car.

When he's gone, I glance at Callie as she plops on the freshly installed porch swing. I watch her swing, smiling with a light laugh as she pats the space beside her. "Do you want to sit? Give it a *swing*."

I huff in frustration, shaking my head, earning me another beautiful smile and giggle from her. I gesture toward her cabin. "Duke mentioned the oven stopped working."

She nods, continuing to enjoy her porch swing. "Yeah, I don't know what happened. It just stopped working a few weeks ago."

"I've got time tomorrow morning to take a look."

"What time?" she asks.

"Whenever works for you."

She raises a brow with a playful smile. "Well, I was hoping to sleep in on a Sunday. Assuming this jerk who cranks up a chainsaw before seven in the morning doesn't perform a repeat wake-up call."

I ignore her comment. "My brother is coming over at noon to decide how we'll be clearing out these bigger trees. There shouldn't be any need for a noise complaint by that time."

She glances at the partially cleared, taped-off property next to her cabin. "Why are you clearing the trees?"

"Adding another cabin," I grumble. "Does 0900 work for you? Gives me time to get parts or a replacement if needed."

"That's fine." She smiles, and I turn away to head to my cabin when she says, "Sure you don't want to try out the new swing? She's swinging like a dream." She sing-songs with a giggle.

I glance at her, lifting my chin to her Jeep. "Move your car and turn the wheels so they're straight. You'll fuck up your drive shaft if you keep leaving it like that."

She swings high, sending me a mocking salute. "Yes, sir."

And if the sight of her beaming smile or the sound of her laughter didn't send a jolt to my cold heart—knowing how happy she is right now because of a damn swing would do the trick.

Four.

Beau

I land three heavy knocks on Callie's front door and wait.

"Coming," she calls just before the chain lock *slides* and the deadbolt *clicks*. The door swings inward to reveal her clad in what I can only describe as *women's torture apparel*—and by all means, is the torture directed solely on *me*.

This woman and her damnable silken sleep sets.

"Good morning," she beams, far more chipper than yesterday's early wakeup call.

"Morning," I grunt as she waves me inside, having to shoo Hulk from his firm stance by the door to allow me in. He follows me to the kitchen, far calmer today versus our first encounter.

"Sorry for the mess," Callie says, rushing ahead as my gaze scans the space.

I didn't get to look around much the other day, given the circumstances, but the place is much smaller than I remember. No wonder Ma said this cabin doesn't get booked as often.

The mess she hurries over to are stacks of papers cluttered across the dining table. An open laptop, an empty coffee mug, and a half-eaten omelet are among the piles of what I'm assuming is...work? What *does* she do exactly?

Not that I care, of course.

I push aside my curiosity and turn my attention toward the stove. The top is still warm from her breakfast and I opt to start with turning on the preheat for the oven to see what happens, if anything.

"It doesn't get to temp," her soft tone announces behind me. I spare a glance over my shoulder as she perches on one of the dining chairs, her slender ankles crossed and tucked beneath her as she closes her computer. "It'll warm up, but nothing over two hundred degrees."

With that new bit of information, I diagnose the problem right away—the heating elements have gone bad. I turn off the oven and tug it away from the wall, searching for the model number to price out replacements.

"Do I need a new one?"

My brow furrows when I glance over my shoulder again to find her standing behind me. She peers around me as I use my phone to take a picture of the metal plate on the back of the stove. The pebbled silk fabric of her top draws my attention, and I'm momentarily mesmerized by the perfect outline of her hardened nipples.

I straighten. "No," I say far too quickly with a shove of my phone into my pocket.

Her expressive eyes widen, taking on a sort of…sultry plea I'm not at all prepared for.

"Well, I mean, it would be kind of nice to get some updated appliances in here," she says sweetly, batting her lashes at me.

My gaze narrows. "It's a bad heating element. Easily replaceable."

At my tone, she pouts. "Okay, but… What if we split the cost?"

"Of what?"

"A new stove." She gestures to the current one beside me. "That thing is like a hundred years old. And, yeah, the stovetop still works, but it's…ugly."

I press my thigh against the front of the 'ugly' oven door and give it a hard shove, forcing it back into place. "If you think using your feminine wiles are going to get you a new stove, you're barking up the wrong tree," I state, pivoting on my heel and heading for the door.

"My feminine *wiles*?" she squawks, following closely. "What are you, ninety? All I want is a new stove. Preferably stainless steel to match the microwave and fridge."

"I'll be back in an hour with replacement parts," I deadpan, ignoring her request.

"But I wa—"

The door slams shut behind me, cutting her off.

I smirk.

❧

I get back to the cabin around 1100 hours with no parts in hand. After three hardware stores across two counties told me they no longer carry elements for the year I need, I was forced to order them online. Not a big deal, I suppose, but I hate leaving a project incomplete.

Or admitting my tenant may need a new stove in the near future...

Rhett's waiting for me when I pulled my truck into the extended driveway. I texted him the specs for the new cabin earlier today and told him to put my lumber order in sooner rather than later.

Unless there was an issue with my numbers, there's no reason he should be here.

He stands at the base of Callie's overly floral porch, chatting with her. I frown at my brother's wide grin as Callie throws her head back laughing at whatever he said that was funny enough to get a reaction like that out of her.

I kill the engine and get out of the truck, heading their way.

"Hey, man," my brother says, smiling like a moron. "How did the parts run go? Callie was just telling me you figured out what's wrong with the oven."

"He did." She crosses her arms, eyeing me proudly. "You're looking a little empty-handed there, Montgomery. Trouble finding the ancient elements?"

Her sassy tone hits me square in the chest, and I fight hard not to give in to her obvious goading. At least she isn't standing out here with my brother in her fucking pajamas. She's changed into a pair of black fitted shorts, a loose white T-shirt, sneakers, and a light grey sweater tied around her waist. She smiles from under the rim of her teal baseball cap.

Rhett's chuckles die in his throat once he takes in the clear annoyance on my face.

"The replacement parts will be here in a few weeks," I tell her, then look to my brother. "Did you need something?"

Rhett scratches the back of his neck. "Can't a guy check in on his brother once in a while?"

I grunt. *No.*

Callie picks up the backpack sitting on her swing. "He really is a ball of sunshine, isn't he?" she comments, tugging the straps over her shoulders.

My brother chuckles awkwardly, glancing between the two of us.

"Where are you going?" I ask, hating how accusatory I sound. What the hell do I care where she's going at eleven o'clock on a Sunday?

"On a hike," she says, Hulk at her side as she descends the few porch steps.

I stare at her choice of footwear. *Fucking tennis shoes.* For a hike on some of the steeper trails around here, that could be seen as a deadly mistake. "You should be wearing proper hiking boots," I tell her sternly. "They're taller to help support your ankles. You'll twist yourself up in those things."

She pauses, raising a single delicate brow. "Now you're going to tell me what I should and shouldn't wear?" She scoffs. "You're unbelievable. Is it that difficult for you to mind your own business?"

I scowl. "I'm trying to help you."

"Yeah, right." She rolls her eyes, walking past me as she waves to my brother, adding, "Good luck with Mr. Sunshine."

"Nice chatting with you," Rhett calls.

I watch her go, feeling more frustrated than I have in years. She claims I can't mind my own business, but why the hell can't she listen to the sound advice I'm trying to give her? She may be proving to be a pain in my ass, but that doesn't mean I want to see her get hurt.

"You two seem...friendly," Rhett says, breaking into my thoughts with that knowing tone of his. The same one he's used since we were kids. He's always had this way of reading people when they don't want to be read.

I face him. "What do you need, Rhett?"

He holds his hands up in surrender. "Just wanted to let you know your lumber order is in. Should be delivered by Wednesday."

He leans against the porch railing and studies me with that irritating smirk. "So, you wanna tell me what that was all about?"

"What do you mean?" I walk past him toward the pile of stakes I set out this morning to mark the water lines. I need to shift my focus before I risk a glance in the direction Callie disappeared to in front of my nosey brother.

"That." He gestures vaguely to my tenant's cabin. "You practically growled over her shoes. Since when do you care what people wear hiking?"

"I don't." My tone comes out sharper than I intended.

Thankfully, instead of giving me shit, he chuckles. "Right. That's why you were glaring at her like she stole one of your beloved power bars."

I ignore his obvious prying and pick up the stakes, setting them where I want them.

"So, how is it going out here, really? I mean, I know you only just got in a few days ago, but... You've been pretty quiet lately."

I've always been quiet. "Fine. Busy."

An amicable silence falls between us. Out of all my siblings, Rhett's been the easiest to talk to. Not that I'm *choosing* to talk to him right now.

Rhett clears his throat, never one to leave silence unfilled. "So, speaking of projects... You free next weekend?"

I glance over my shoulder, eyeing him suspiciously. "Why?"

"Glad you asked." He grins. "Since Butch and Duke decided to do this double wedding thing—me, being the genius brother I am, thought: Hey, let's hit this double-thing over the head and do a bachelor party for the two of them."

I stare at him.

"It'll be great."

Doesn't sound great to me.

"Next Saturday at Tavern Nine. Beer, poker, the whole brother bonding experience. Dad's stopping by, Uncle Jim, some young guns from Butch's company." He chuckles. "Should be a riot."

Should be a nightmare is more like it, but there isn't much I can do to get out of this one. "I'll be there," I say begrudgingly.

"You better be," he says. "I'd hate to have to show up here and tear you away from..." He gestures vaguely at Callie's cabin, then at me. "Whatever this is."

My brow furrows.

At my glare, he adds, "Just saying what I see, bro."

"Don't bother," I deadpan, already hating whatever the hell nonsense he's mentally brewing over the single encounter he witnessed between Callie and me.

He laughs, waving me off as he strides to his truck. "I'll see you later at Ma's for dinner." He starts the engine. Rolling down the window, he shouts, "And Beau? Maybe ease up on the shoe policing. Most women don't take kindly to that kind of mountain man safety flirting."

I flip him off, which just makes him laugh harder as he backs out of the driveway.

As his truck disappears down the road, I find myself glancing toward the trail where Callie vanished earlier. *Tennis shoes*. I shake my head to clear her from my thoughts and get to work.

The next morning, however, she's gone.

Five.

Callie

"Try the sheer bodice one next," my best friend, Shea, calls from outside her closet in her ocean-side condo here in Long Beach.

"I wore red last time, though," I say, eyeing the five dress options she has me choosing from today. I'm on the hunt for a dress for the upcoming premiere of the final chapter in my *Devil's Lake* movie trilogy. And whenever I need to dress for the red carpet, Shea is my go-to and well worth a trip back to California.

We met in college. She went for fashion and design while I was studying film and photography. We ran into each other one day on campus during the first week of classes. She complimented my flats while complaining about her heels killing her feet. We swapped shoes—which we laugh about now as being gross and far too trustworthy—and the rest was history.

Ten years later, her opinion is still the only one I've ever taken to heart.

She's the reason I moved from sunny Los Angeles to a little remote cabin in the mountains of Whitetail. It was her idea, given her father owns the infamous Winton's Resort on the other side of the small town. She knew I needed the break. I wasn't in the right headspace to be making any major decisions on my own. And I trust her.

Something that doesn't come easily for me.

Shea pops her head around the corner, her bouncy ringlet curls framing her face and complementing her rich, brown complexion. "And you looked hot as hell," she retorts. "So stop whining and try it on."

I groan sarcastically, earning a laugh from her as she slips into her bedroom to await another failed model walk by yours truly. "I was thinking something more dramatic this time," I say, running my fingers along the fabric of the sheer red gown with subtle silver threading. "Something that says 'final chapter' without being too on-the-nose about it."

Shea hums from the other room. "Well, you know I love dramatic looks. And you *have* poured fifteen years of your life into this trilogy."

Has it been that long?

I started writing short horror films for YouTube with some friends in high school—none of them took it as seriously as I did. From there, my little hobby grew and never stopped. It wasn't until I was in college that the short films began to take off. I got recognized by one of my professors, who then introduced me to some huge-name producers in the horror genre.

One day, I was showing them my latest screenplay with safety pins holding my purse together, and the next...I'm cashing checks worth millions.

I shimmy into the dress, having to hold the strapless breast cups to my chest as I shuffle out of the closet. I smile at the sight of Shea sitting on the edge of her bed to pet Hulk sleeping soundly on the bulk of it. "Zip assist, please."

"Oooh." Shea whistles when I offer my back to her so she can secure the dress. "Your body in this dress is stunning, Cals. Seriously."

I step toward her floor-to-ceiling mirror in the corner of the room and take in the full-length gown. It has a true mermaid style fit to it and complements my figure in more ways than one. I turn to the side and inspect the back. "I don't love the silver accents or the red, but this shape is perfect."

"Pause!" Shea leaps to her feet, scurrying to the closet before emerging with a similar vibe to the current dress I'm wearing. A sheer corseted, mermaid sequined gown, exquisite beads and crystals with a high slit design in a dusty pink. "What about this one? It has that rich, haunting vibe that matches the *Devil's* aesthetic."

I can't help but smile. This is why I love Shea. She doesn't just see clothes; she sees stories, moods, statements. While I was at my writing desk trying to capture the mysterious waters of *Devil's Lake* that made the trilogy such a hit, she was building her reputation as one of the most intuitive stylists in the industry.

"I don't know what I'd do without you." I hurry past her, taking the dress as I do.

"Probably show up in sweats and a tank top," she teases.

I laugh, changing into the new dress that is much easier to get into by myself and has thin spaghetti straps. It needs to be taken in a smidge at the waist, but Shea will have it ready for me before the premiere in six weeks. "No nip slips this year, I'm afraid," I say as I walk out of the closet and head for the mirror.

"Oh god. Remember your first premiere?" A nostalgic smile plays on her lips as she laughs. "You were so nervous. I thought you were going to flash the cameras on purpose just to get it over with."

I snort. "I'm shocked that dress didn't do it for me." I turn several times and test sitting before announcing, "This is it. I love it, Shea. You hit it out of the park once again."

My best friend squeals, waking Hulk with a start. "Sorry, big boy," she coos, petting his head before returning her attention to me. "Unfortunately, I don't have any shoes to go with that dress, so..."

I roll my eyes. *So* unfortunate. "Yes, we can go shopping tomorrow," I agree. Shea beams. "I have to meet with Nathan to go over some last-minute security for the after party, but I should be free by noon."

"Lunch and shoe shopping it is," she says, but her smile quickly falters. "Wait. Did you say *security*? Did something happen?"

Worry etches into her face and I shake my head. "No. I mean, not...yet."

Shea sighs. "Callie."

"Don't waste your breath." I spin and sashay my way into the closet to change into my clothes, hoping she'll let it go, but she never does. "I'd rather be safe than sorry," I call out. The cliché makes me sound like my father, but it's not a lie in the slightest.

I've been sorry more than once in the last nine years.

"I understand that, but it's been over a year," she says from the other room. "The police caught the bastard. He's rotting in some jail cell—hopefully with some other asshole who stinks to high heaven making his measly life even worse."

I come out in my high-waisted denim shorts and tank. "I know."

"We went over the statistics."

"I know."

"You said that was enough."

"And it...was," I admit with a sigh, recalling Shea's excessive amount of Googling that day when we learned one in twelve women are a victim of stalking at least once in their lifetime.

Unfortunately for me, I've had three...

The first one was in high school. A friend of a friend who thought it'd be fun to hack into my webcam and watch me from my computer. Thankfully, that got shut down rather quickly, but it was almost a year before he stopped following me around school.

The second was in college. A bitter ex-boyfriend who refused to let go for two years, regardless of the restraining orders or threats from my father.

And the most recent...a crazed fan. I've gotten hate mail to marriage proposals, but this was different than anything I'd dealt with in the past. He broke into my apartment. He left messages on the walls with ideas on how the *Devil's* trilogy should end. There were pictures of me hanging on the doors of coffee shops I frequented. My clothes went missing, vases of flowers would appear in random rooms, my phone—no matter how many times I changed the number—would ring with no one on the other end.

I moved around, living between Shea's and my father's, terrified to stay in one place for too long. That was when I met Hulk. Dad called in a few favors and got Hulk certified quickly at my therapist's recommendation. She called it 'extreme paranoia' while my dad claimed PTSD.

And when Matthew Ryan sets his mind to something—like Hulk being my 'cure'—there were no legal bounds to keep him from making damn sure his little girl had the constant protection she needed.

One I am more than grateful for.

"You haven't been having any issues in Montana, have you?" Shea asks. "Because if you are, you can come back here and live with me. Or I can talk to my dad and see if we can stay at one of the resorts for a while. You know he cares about you, too."

I'd be lying if I said I didn't miss California—the beach, *not* the people—but Montana is a whole different world. The people are kinder, the weather grants you all four seasons, and the beauty of the mountains is unmatched.

I smile faintly. "Whitetail has been good to me so far. And I haven't had any issues, really. I mean, other than my grumpy landlord."

"Duke?"

"No, his brother. Beau." I scrunch my nose at the very thought of our last encounter and his gripe over my choice of footwear.

Shea smirks. "Ah, yes, the big, muscly soldier with the nice chest hair."

I burst out laughing. "Is that all you took from that conversation?" I ask, plopping on the bed beside her and falling against the sea of pillows. "I say one thing about a guy's chest—"

She turns to me, her legs crossed beneath her. "Do *not* downplay this for me," she states, a glint in her eye. "I haven't heard you talk about a guy in *any* capacity for... Tell me, are there cobwebs in your cave of wonders or just dust?"

I snatch the pillow from behind my head and whip it in her direction. "Stop!"

We laugh for a few minutes over vagina innuendos before our laughter subsides.

Shea moves closer to me, her expression serious. "I worry about you, Cals. When I suggested you get away, I didn't think you'd be gone this long. I miss you."

I sit up at the emotion in her voice. "I miss you, too," I say, pulling her in for a hug. She gives me a light squeeze. "I'm okay. I promise. It's just..." I trail off and Hulk perks up, his gaze finding mine. "It's this place, Shea. Fame is not for me. I love what I do, don't get me wrong, but the *obsession* people have here... It's too much."

"I get that," she says, brushing a tear from her cheek.

"You can come see me, too, you know," I offer, taking her hand. "There's plenty of cute mountain men just waiting to grovel at your feet."

She smirks. "So now he's cute?"

I rush to say, "I never said—"

"If I didn't know any better," she's full-blown beaming now, "I'd think you have a crush, Miss Hot-Shot Movie Director slash Screenwriter Extraordinaire."

I fight to contain any form of a smile and aim for disgust. "Ew. Gross."

Shea rolls her eyes, laughing. "Uh-huh. Whatever you say."

We spend the rest of the day catching up after six months apart. Opting to stay in, we order takeout, watch Real Housewives, laugh, and gossip. The whole time, a certain grumpy veteran lingers in the back of my mind, and I find myself wondering what he's doing...and if he's thinking about me, too.

Six.

Beau

"BEAU? YOU OUT HERE, son?" my father calls from outside the shed.

I grit my teeth. "Yeah. In here."

I've spent the last three days and two nights at my parents' house, sleeping in my childhood bedroom on a twin-sized mattress that has my feet dangling off the end and my knee killing me every damn morning.

The old metal shelves creak when I push aside boxes labeled in my mother's neat handwriting. Camping gear, Christmas decorations, old sports equipment—all catalogued and preserved like family artifacts. That's my mother for you, keeping everything just in case one of us might need it someday.

Dad appears in the doorway, blocking what little light filters into the musty shed. "Your mother's been calling you. Dinner is ready."

"I'll be there in a minute," I mutter, shoving another box aside.

He doesn't leave. Instead, he steps inside, the floorboards groaning under his weight. "What are you looking for?"

"My old tent." I don't look at him as I continue my search. "The small one. Two-person Coleman."

"Going camping?" he asks. His tone is casual, but I know my father. Nothing he asks is without purpose.

I don't respond.

He's quiet for a moment, watching me rummage through piles of junk that should've been thrown out years ago. "Your mother put all the camping gear in the rafters after you left. Said there wasn't much point keeping it accessible with you overseas."

I glance up at the wooden beams above us, spotting the edge of a plastic storage bin. Of course. I ignore the twinge in my knee and reach up.

That bed may have fucked me up more than I thought.

"I can get that," Dad offers.

"I got it," I grunt.

The bin is heavier than it looks, and as I maneuver it down, pain shoots through my bad knee. I clench my jaw, refusing to show it.

"So," Dad says when I set the bin on the floor and pop open the lid. "You thinking of sleeping at your property before the cabin's built?"

I find the tent bag buried beneath a tangle of camp stoves and lanterns. "That's the plan."

"It's supposed to rain."

"I've slept in worse."

Dad huffs, a sound I've heard a thousand times. Disappointment, concern, resignation—all wrapped in a single exhale. "Your mother's not going to like it."

Nothing I can do about that.

"She worries about you. We all do." He leans against the doorframe, crossing his arms. "You only just got back, son."

I stuff the tent into its bag, along with a rolled-up sleeping pad. "I've been stateside for months."

"In DC. Not here."

He's really not wanting to let this go. He can see how miserable I've been here—crowded by everyone, waited on like I'm a fucking child. I got here Sunday, thinking I could handle a week of family before the bachelor party next weekend. Now here it is, Tuesday evening, and I've wanted to rip my hair out since Sunday.

"I need my own space." I zip the bag closed with more force than necessary. I debate telling him part of the truth is I can't sleep on that damn bed another night, but then he'll ask about my knee, he'll tell Ma, then I'll really be aggravated.

Dad nods slowly. "I understand that."

"Good," I say, hefting the tent bag over my shoulder.

He watches me, heavy with the weight of all the things he wants to say. The questions he wants to ask about what happened overseas, my knee, why I've barely spoken ten words at dinner each night. But he doesn't ask. That's not how my father operates.

Instead, he says, "Let's head inside. Dinner's getting cold."

I follow him out of the shed. The tent bag bumps against my back with each step, a small victory in my quiet rebellion. I'll eat my mother's casserole and deflect her questions about my plans. I'll sit through my sister, Lily, yapping about some modeling agent that contacted her through Instagram and hear more details about my brothers' wedding than any man should.

Because tonight, I'll be on my property. Alone. A nylon barrier between myself and the rest of the world.

Just the way I like it.

I jolt awake when a stream of ice-cold water hits my face. For a disoriented moment, I think I'm back overseas, huddled in a leaking transport while monsoon season wreaks havoc. Then I remember, I'm in a fucking tent on my property, and my brilliant plan is quite literally underwater.

Thunder cracks overhead, vibrating through the ground beneath my soaked sleeping bag. I reach for my phone. It's 0117. The dim light reveals what I already know. Everything is drenched. My duffel, my boots—all of it submerged in the inch of water that's pooled beneath my sleeping pad turned waterbed.

"Goddammit," I growl, struggling to sit up.

My knee screams in protest as I shift positions, the cold amplifying the ever-present ache to a sharp stab of pain. Two nights in this tent had been manageable. When it was dry, mind you. Now, with rain coming down hard enough to sound like machine-gun fire against the nylon shell, the situation has become unbearable.

Another leak springs open above me, this one dumping water directly onto my chest. I grab my phone and duffel, knowing there's no salvaging this night.

I haven't been this wet and miserable since training exercises in Georgia.

Unzipping the tent flap, I'm greeted by a downpour. The rain hammers against the earth with enough force to bounce back up, creating a fog of water at ground level. My worksite is a mud pit, the stakes I'd carefully placed now barely visible in puddles of rust-colored water.

I make a break for my truck, my bad leg tense as I slog through the muck. By the time I reach the driver's side door, any inch of me that *was* dry isn't anymore. I'm soaked to the bone, my T-shirt and sweats clinging to me like a second layer of misery.

Inside the truck, I crank the heat as high as it'll go, but it does little to cut through the bone-deep chill. I stare through the fogged windshield toward my useless tent, now partially collapsed under the weight of the water.

Now what?

I could drive to my parents' house. Ma would let me in without question, would probably even have fresh towels and hot coffee ready within minutes. But the thought of their concern, the questions, the inevitable '*I told you so*' hanging unspoken in the air—I can't stomach it. Not tonight.

My gaze drifts to Callie's cabin. Dark. Silent. She'd left at the crack of dawn Monday morning without a word, and she hasn't been home since. The warm, dry house sits empty, mocking me with its solid walls and waterproof roof.

I can't.

I shouldn't...

As another crack of thunder shakes my truck and rain hammers harder against the windows, my resolve begins to crumble.

It's one night.

No one would know.

I'll sleep on the couch and set an alarm.

I'll leave the house exactly as is—*no one* will be the wiser.

Decision made, I grab my duffel and make a run for her porch. The stairs are slippery, nearly sending me sprawling as my bad knee buckles slightly. *Fuck.* I catch myself on the railing, cursing under my breath.

Under the protection of her porch overhang, I dig through my bag for the spare key Duke gave me. The door opens with a creak, and I step into the dark interior of the cabin. It smells like her—floral mixed with fresh linens and honey.

It's intoxicating.

I breathe easier as I find the switch on the wall, flooding the entryway with warm light. "Breaking and entering. Nice," I mutter to no one, leaving my muddy boots by the door.

The cabin is eerily quiet without her presence, the constant soundtrack of her god-awful music, or talking to her oversized dog. I stand dripping on her entry rug, suddenly unsure of myself.

This is crossing a line.

And a law or two.

But as water puddles around my feet, practicality wins out over propriety. *I'll clean up after myself*, I repeat. *She'll never know I was here*.

And I do need to warm up before my knee locks completely.

I step farther inside, navigating toward the bathroom attached to the single bedroom—*her* bedroom. The bathroom light flickers on, revealing my reflection in the mirror. I look like hell. Three days of stubble, dark circles under my eyes. I strip off my soaked clothes and hang them over the shower rod to dry, then pause.

A shower wasn't part of the plan, but...

I turn the knob and wait for the hot water to kick in. The water pressure is surprisingly good, and steam quickly fills the small space. Stepping under the spray, the heat penetrates my frozen muscles, bringing painful pins and needles as circulation returns.

There is only one bottle of body wash on the shower ledge. Something with a purple label claiming to be lavender and sea salt. I hesitate for a moment. I've already invaded her home, her privacy. What's some borrowed soap going to hurt at this point?

The scent is decidedly feminine as I work it into a lather. I'm flooded with thoughts of a certain honey-blonde woman, curves, and a supple ass.

By the time I shut off the water, my skin is red and the throbbing in my knee has shifted to a different area of my body.

I reach for a towel from the rack and find myself holding the fluffiest, pinkest monstrosity I've ever seen. *Of course, she would have pink towels.* I shake my head and dry off before wrapping it around my waist, leaving my clothes to continue drying.

I really ought to consider installing laundry for the third cabin.

I exit the bathroom into her bedroom and pause at the threshold. I should head straight for the couch—that was the plan, anyhow—but curiosity gets the better of me as I take in the space that is undeniably *hers.*

A quilt in shades of teal and violet covers the neatly made bed, piled with more pillows than any one person could possibly need. Books are stacked on both nightstands; their spines creased from multiple readings. A pair of glasses rests atop one pile, and I'm surprised. I've never seen her wear them.

Framed photographs line the dresser. Callie with an older man who shares her smile—her father, I presume. Callie on a mountainside, arms spread wide with Hulk sitting at her feet. Callie with a group of women, all holding wine glasses and laughing.

No younger men in any of the photos.

Why the hell did I need to notice that?

I'm intruding. Not just in her home, but in her private world. The realization sits uncomfortably in my chest as I force myself to walk through the room without touching anything.

The living room is warm even without a fire in the hearth. The couch is deep and soft, covered in a patchwork throw that looks handmade. I sink onto it, the exhaustion of the past few days catching up to me all at once. The rain continues its assault outside, but in here everything is still and peaceful.

I should set that alarm, make sure I'm gone at first light. I try to remember where I set my phone, but my eyelids are already growing heavy.

Just five minutes of rest, then I'll get up and...

A low, threatening growl pulls me from the depths of sleep.

Seven.

Callie

THE GRAVEL DRIVEWAY IS a mess. More mud than road after last night's apparent downpour. I navigate my Jeep around the worst of it, the headlights cutting through the predawn darkness to reveal a landscape transformed. Fallen branches litter the yard. My flower beds are decimated, petals and stems pasted to the dirt like a sad collage.

"I'm glad we didn't have to fly through that storm," I murmur to Hulk sitting perch in the passenger seat.

The short trip to LA was a success. After party and premiere details were set, security was booked, I got to view the final chapter in my movie trilogy for the fifth time, and I spent five days hanging out with my best friend. It's safe to say I'm feeling much more confident about traveling for the upcoming premiere.

Although I'm not looking forward to spending the two weeks doing promotions and interviews, but none of that starts for another month.

As I pull closer to the cabin, something unexpected catches my eye near Beau's little construction site. A half-collapsed tent, sagging under the weight of pooled rainwater.

That's...odd.

I frown, putting the car in park. I reach for my phone and check the time. 6:23 AM. Too early to call said grumpy landlord and ask what's going on. I shoot him a text, expecting a response in another hour or so.

I hop out of the car, and my sneakers slap the driveway with a splash of mud. Fantastic.

"You be careful," I tell Hulk, opening the passenger door. "Don't get too muddy or you'll need a bath."

He leaps down, on alert as he surveys our surroundings. I decide to get Hulk his breakfast before I return to grab my bags. He was so patient on the early morning flight. Together we walk up the porch steps as I remove my keys to open the door and...

I freeze.

The door is unlocked. The deadbolt no longer engaged.

My heart jumps into my throat.

I *always* lock my door. Always.

Memories flash through my mind—shattered glass, drawers emptied, belongings scattered, the violation that followed me across California and into my nightmares.

"*Such*," I whisper to Hulk, the search command we've practiced hundreds of times.

He moves, nose to the door seam, his body tense. A low growl builds in his chest—not his warning for everyday strangers. This is his alert.

Someone is inside.

My hands shake as I pull out my phone, my finger hovering over the emergency call button. I should back away, call for help, wait in my car with the doors locked. That's what my father would tell me to do. Safe. Logical.

But this is my home.

One I've worked very hard to make mine over the last six months. It's my safe place.

And someone has invaded it.

With trembling fingers, I grip the doorknob. It turns with a *click* that sounds obscenely loud in the quiet early morning. Hulk's growl deepens when I push the door open slowly, my other hand still clutching my phone. The cabin is dark except for the faint glow of sunlight beaming in through the far windows.

I try to steady my breathing despite the fear coursing through me. I can *feel* a disturbance in the air, a subtle wrongness that prickles the hair on my arms. I reach for the light switch and turn it on, flooding the main living space with sudden brightness.

That's when I see them—muddy boots by the door. Men's work boots.

My breath catches.

Hulk moves forward, his body a barrier between me and whatever awaits. His hackles are raised, teeth bared in silent threat as he stalks forward. My legs feel leaden as I follow him, every instinct screaming at me to run, but I force myself to stay, one hand buried in Hulk's fur for courage.

The couch comes into view, and there, sprawled across it, is a man.

And not just any man.

Beau Montgomery.

For a moment, my fear gives way to relief, then to utter confusion. Beau's asleep on my couch, one arm flung over his eyes, the other dangling toward the floor with his knee propped up on a pillow. His chest rises and falls in the deep rhythm of an exhausted sleep.

He's shirtless. Wearing nothing but one of my pink bath towels wrapped around his hips.

I blink rapidly, trying to process what I'm seeing. My grumpy, perpetually scowling landlord is asleep naked on my couch at six in the morning.

"*Steh platz,*" I whisper, letting Hulk know he can stand down. He reluctantly backs up, but remains on high alert, his gaze fixed on Beau.

I take a moment to study him. The carved plains of his chest, arms...legs. His left knee, I've seen him wear a brace over, is bare and savagely scarred. Jagged skin and burn marks sit alongside clean lines that appear surgical in nature. My gaze flicks to his chest where a few scars mar his toned torso, weaving through his thick-cut abs.

He stirs slightly in his sleep, shifting his weight on the cushions. The arm covering his eyes falls away, revealing his face and peaceful expression, so different from his usual constipated scowl. His strong jaw is relaxed, and his full lips part slightly. Without the usual furrow between his brows, he looks younger. Vulnerable.

My gaze shifts downward once again, tracing the defined ridges of his abdomen, the bulky cut of his hips, and the way my pink towel contrasts with his tanned skin. The fabric has loosened with his movement, slipping lower on one hip and exposing more of that V-line.

It should be illegal for men like Beau to show their Vs in public.

I can't help but notice the distinct bulge beneath the towel, the fabric tented slightly. Heat floods my cheeks and a warmth races down my spine, settling low in my belly. I swallow hard, very aware of how intimate this moment is.

Hulk chooses said moment to growl at our intruder. His low warning breaks the spell. Beau's eyes fly open—alert and focused despite his abrupt waking.

His gaze lands on Hulk and he bolts upright, disorientation clear on his face for a split second before his gaze locks with mine. I watch comprehension dawn, followed by something I've never seen on him before. Embarrassment.

"What are you doing in my house?" My voice comes out steadier than I feel, riding on a wave of relief and...something else I'm not ready to admit.

Hulk growls again, a second warning that needs no translation. I keep my hand firmly on his collar, but I don't call him off completely.

Beau runs a hand through his short, sleep-mussed hair. The movement causes the towel to slip even lower on his hips. I force my focus to remain locked on his face, refusing to acknowledge the direction that towel is heading.

"Callie," he says, his voice rough from sleep. "You weren't here."

Of all the things he could have said, that is probably the worst. Like it would have been fine if I hadn't caught him? Is he serious?

"That's not even close to an explanation," I say.

Hulk shifts beside me, sensing my increased emotions. It's hard to say if I'm leaning more toward anger, fear, or worry at this point.

Beau eyes Hulk warily, but to his credit, he doesn't flinch.

"The storm," he finally says, gesturing toward the window. "My tent—"

"You broke into my home because it was raining?" The absurdity of it almost makes me laugh.

"I didn't *break* in," he counters weakly. "I used the key Duke gave me."

The spare key that should only be used if I *lose* mine and because Duke *was* my landlord. I can get past Beau having it now, considering he *is* my current landlord, but this? "That's for emergencies! Like a busted water pipe, or if I can't get into the house. Not for—" I wave my hand at his state of undress, at the clear evidence that he's made himself right at home in my absence. "—whatever this is."

The bold reality of the situation hits me full force. He's been in my bathroom. Used my shower. Touched my things. Slept in my space without permission. The boundaries I've so carefully constructed feel tampered with. Shattered.

Never mind that he's a familiar face with a hot—and albeit tempting—well-built physique.

I'm mad now. Mad and hurt and...

Beau's expression shifts from defensive to concerned as he grips the edge of his towel and stands. His towering stature and defined chest a mere foot away. "Callie," he says, softer this time. "You're shaking."

I am. My whole body trembles with a mixture of emotions I can't begin to process. *Just when I thought I could let my guard down.* I press my lips together to keep them from quivering and take a step back. Hulk moves with me. "Get dressed," I manage to say. "And get out."

Something flickers across Beau's face. Regret, maybe? He gives a single, silent nod before turning toward the bedroom and into the bathroom. His back muscles flex with each step, and I hate that I notice them. The door closes behind him with a soft *click*.

I stand rooted in place, Hulk pressed against my leg for support. A minute later, the door opens. Beau emerges fully dressed in grey sweatpants and an army green T-shirt. He moves with quiet efficiency, gathering his phone from the coffee table, his keys, and a small duffel I hadn't noticed beside the door.

Not once does he look at me.

The morning light catches on his profile, highlighting the tension in his jaw, the rigid set of his shoulders. He pauses at the front door, his hand wrapped around the doorknob. For a heartbeat, I think he might say something to break this painful silence. Apologize, even. But he doesn't. The door opens, and without a backward glance, he steps through and pulls it shut behind him.

I'm alone.

Eight.

Callie

TODAY IS...NOT THE BEST day. I didn't sleep for the second night in a row. I'm running on sheer frustration and short naps throughout the day if I can manage to fall asleep. It's been twenty-four hours since I caught Beau sleeping on my couch. We've both been fairly busy with our own stuff.

Him outside, avoiding eye contact.

Me inside, trying to work on my next big project.

I peek out the front window. Beau is outside, a hammer in hand. A complete lower framework is pieced together between his taped-off stakes. God knows how long he's been awake for to have made so much progress since yesterday.

He's shirtless, drenched in sweat, and chugging a bottle of water that has the thick cords of his neck flexing and straining.

He removes the rim from his lips and splashes his face with the remaining bit of water. My thighs clamp together when he rubs one meaty paw over his face and into his hair.

Hulk nudges my hand, indicating he needs to go out. I'm brought back to reality and attempt not to read *too* far into the ease in my shoulders compared to a moment ago.

It has nothing to do with the grumpy army veteran working and living *outside my front door. Nope, none.*

Although, I don't know where he's been sleeping since I kicked him off my couch. Where he slept last night...I haven't got a clue.

After I let Hulk out back to do his business, I serve him breakfast and make myself some oatmeal. I work on a few scenes for a current screenplay between getting ready for the day and cleaning. I opt for a light lunch and give Hulk one of his chewy sticks to keep him occupied.

It's after two o'clock when I start to get flustered by the direction my manuscript has taken. "He can't kill her this early," I mutter to myself, gnawing my pen cap in thought. An awful habit I picked up during a writing course in college.

My head falls back on a heavy sigh, and Hulk perks up from his dog bed by the sofa.

I smile when his tail flops three times. "Walkies?" My buddy is up on his feet, stretching a second later. I stand, too, hoping the activity will tire me out enough to sleep for longer than a few hours tonight. "Glad we're in agreement."

I change my clothes into my usual hiking attire and clip Hulk into his harness before packing a few water bottles, treats, and granola bars into my backpack.

We're out the door in five minutes, passing Beau on our way to the hiking trail down the road. I idly note his pause to watch me. Given I'm wearing the same shoes he had an issue with before, I'd venture to say he's biting his tongue from spouting another lecture on proper footwear.

I snort to myself. Wasn't I just thinking he was cute in a grumpy, overbearing sort of way not too long ago? Clearly, I'm delusional.

Hulk and I reach the trailhead we've hiked over a dozen times. The trail moves up the mountain, winding through the trees for a quarter mile before it forks into three different directions. We've done the two lower-level trails, which according to the sign, are easy to moderate in difficulty, while the third is listed as challenging and strenuous.

"What'll it be, bud?" I ask Hulk. "I wouldn't mind a challenge today. How 'bout you?" Having to stay focused on the hike would help me get out of my head. "Come on. This way," I say, patting my thigh for Hulk to follow as I branch off straight ahead.

The challenging trail lives up to its name right away. The path narrows and steepens, forcing me to watch each step carefully. Exposed roots crisscross the dirt like nature's tripwires. Hulk navigates the terrain with enviable ease, his paws finding purchase where my running shoes occasionally slip on the loose earth.

"Show-off," I mutter.

He turns his head, tongue lolling in his signature doggy grin.

An hour into the hike, the forest begins to thin. The air feels crisper in my lungs. Sweat trickles down my spine despite the cool morning, and my calves burn from exertion. This is exactly what I needed—a physical challenge to drown out the noise.

The path curves around a massive boulder, and the world opens before us.

"Oh, wow," I breathe, coming to a stop.

We've reached a rocky outcrop that juts from the mountainside like a natural viewing platform. Below us stretches a panoramic view that steals my breath. The valley unfolds in a patchwork of emerald and gold. The mountains beyond rise in waves of blue-grey, each range fainter than the last until they dissolve into the horizon.

"Hulk, look at this," I whisper, though he's already standing at attention, ears perked as he takes in the vast expanse before us.

I like to think he appreciates these views and our little adventures as much as I do.

I ease my pack off and retrieve a water bottle. I pour half into a travel bowl I keep in my bag for him before sipping the second half while I settle on a flat rock. Hulk laps at his bowl, then sits beside me. Out here, my anxieties and worries seem so small. So manageable.

The wind whispers through the pines, carrying the scent of earth and rain. A hawk circles lazily overhead, its piercing cry echoing across the valley. I close my eyes for a moment, letting the sounds and sensations wash over me.

We stay for nearly half an hour, snacking on a granola bar and dog treats while soaking in the view from every angle. I snap a few photos with my phone, though they can't possibly capture the magic of this spot.

Eventually, I shoulder my pack, wanting to get home before dark. "Time to head back, buddy."

The descent proves trickier than the climb. Gravity pulls at me with each step, making the steep sections treacherous. I move carefully, using nearby tree trunks for balance on the steepest parts. "Slow and steady," I huff.

We're about halfway down when the trail narrows alongside a drop-off I hadn't paid any mind to on the way up. It's not a sheer cliff, but steep enough to be dangerous—a rocky slope dotted with scrub brush falling away for at least thirty feet before leveling out.

I hug the inside of the path, keeping Hulk between me and the mountainside. My foot lands on what looks like solid ground, but proves to be loose rock hidden under a thin layer of dirt.

It happens in an instant.

My ankle twists as the ground gives way. I throw out my arms, desperately grasping for anything stable, but there's nothing but air. Hulk lunges toward me, his training kicking in as he tries to stabilize me, but my momentum is too great. Instead of saving me, he falls with me as we tumble over the edge.

I scream.

We slide, then roll. Sharp rocks tear at my clothes, my skin. I try to protect my head, but I'm spinning, disoriented. Hulk yelps somewhere nearby and I desperately want to reach for him. Pain explodes through my body each time I impact the ground.

Then something hard catches my temple.

Stars burst across my vision.

Then nothing.

Nine.

Beau

Dusk casts a shadow over my property as I break down for the day. Thankfully, the renters in the two-bedroom cabin—a couple in town for a wedding—left a day early, so I'm able to shower and cook myself dinner tonight. I slept well enough in my truck last night, though I have the option to crash in the rental for tonight at least.

I toss my work gloves on the tailgate of my truck and glance at Callie's cabin. I didn't see her come back, but a light is on inside, indicating to me someone must be home.

I guess I missed her.

The double meaning in that statement isn't lost on me.

I want to make this right, is what I want to tell her. Problem is, I'm shit with words and getting them out when I need to. Always have been. Every time I rehearse what I want to say to her, then get the chance to, my head is hollow and the moment passes.

I start packing my tools away methodically, each one finding its designated spot in the bed of my truck. The rhythm of the work is soothing, familiar. Unlike the knot of frustration that tightens in my chest whenever I think about Callie and the mess I've made, the fear in her eyes yesterday.

She'd gone hiking this afternoon. I spotted her and Hulk heading toward the mountain trail with those same flimsy sneakers on her feet that I warned her about. The stubborn woman had just marched past me, chin up, those blonde waves bouncing with each determined step.

I wanted to call out, to say something, *anything*, but the words got stuck in my throat.

Story of my damn life with this woman.

A distant sound catches my attention—a bark followed by a whimper. I straighten, my brow furrowed as I listen intently.

There it is again. More urgent this time.

I turn toward the road and see a shape inching toward me. Limping.

I'd recognize that massive German Shepherd anywhere. Hulk.

But something feels wrong when I peer farther down the road. I don't see Callie. And Hulk is never without her. Never.

I drop the shovel I'm holding and jog toward him. As I get closer, I can see he's favoring his hind legs. There are scratches along his side, dirt and blood mat patches of his fur. He looks like he was just in one hell of a fight.

"Hey, boy," I say, approaching slowly. He and I haven't had the best start, but he's heading straight toward me—and he doesn't look too good. "Where's Callie?"

At the sound of her name, Hulk barks sharply, then turns toward the trail. His gaze shifts to me and he barks once more before limping a few steps in the trail's direction.

My blood runs cold. "Show me."

The sun is fading fast, painting the sky in deep oranges and purples. Not much daylight left. I follow Hulk's limping form down the road, my pace quickening despite the dull ache in my knee as we move up the mountain.

The trailhead looms ahead, three paths branching from the main one. I've hiked them all countless times while surveying the property years ago, but which one did Callie take?

Hulk hesitates at the fork, whining as he looks between the paths.

"Which way?"

He starts toward the center trail—the most difficult one—but stops, circling back with a pained whimper. His injury is slowing him down, and he's clearly in a lot of pain.

I kneel, examining the ground. The recent rain has left the dirt soft enough to hold impressions. There—a distinct footprint heading up the center trail. Small. And beside it, paw prints.

"Stay," I tell Hulk, pointing firmly at the ground. He barks, trying to follow me, but I can't risk him injuring himself further. I need to move fast, and he's in no condition to keep up. "I'll find her. I promise," I say, wondering if he can even understand me.

Sure enough, he lies down at the head of the path with a whimper, his gaze on me.

I set off at a brisk pace, following the most challenging trail. My knee strains with each upward movement, but I ignore it. The trail gets steeper, rockier. The kind of terrain that could be dangerous for someone in inadequate footwear.

"Callie," I call out, my voice echoing through the trees. "Callie, can you hear me?"

Nothing but the rustling of leaves in the evening breeze answers me.

I push on, the light fading by the minute. I scan the path ahead. About a mile in, I spot something that makes my heart stop. A small section of disturbed earth at the edge of the trail, right where it narrows beside a steep drop-off.

"Hulk!" Her scream is terrified. The raw panic in her voice sends adrenaline surging through my veins as I sprint ahead. "Hulk, where are you? Please, baby, answer me."

"Callie," I shout.

Her screams stop abruptly. "Hello? Who's there?"

I slow as I approach the disturbed edge, peering carefully over at the rampage of debris showing signs of a rockslide. About twenty feet down the steep embankment, I spot her—half-sitting against a boulder, blood matting her hair on one side, face streaked with dirt, blood, and tears. Her right leg is stretched in front of her.

Relief washes over me at finding her alive. "Stay still. I'm coming to you." Dirt instantly gives way under my boot and I curse to myself. I opt for a different angle to hopefully avoid any more debris from falling in her direction.

The slope is treacherous—loose shale and dirt mixed with jagged rocks. I sit at the edge and begin to slide down carefully, using my good leg to brace against larger rocks and roots, controlling my descent. Pain shoots through my knee with each jarring movement. I grit my teeth and keep going.

She peers at me. "Beau?" Confusion colors her voice, quickly followed by renewed panic. "Can you see Hulk? I can't find him. He fell with me, but when I woke up...I-I can't—"

"He's okay," I say, carefully picking my way down toward her. "He came to find me."

She stares at me, disbelief battling with hope. "He went for help?"

"Smart dog you've got there," I say as loose rocks cascade down from under my boots. "Fuck."

"Where is he?"

"He's waiting at the trailhead. His back leg's injured, but he managed to make it to me."

Fresh tears spill over her cheeks. "Is he really okay?"

"He will be. Right now, we need to worry about you." I reach her side, crouching to examine her injuries. Up close, the gash on her temple has stopped bleeding but looks nasty. She's going to need stitches. Her ankle is also visibly swollen. "Can you move your toes?"

She nods, demonstrating with a grimace. "Just a sprain, I think. My head hurts worse."

"You probably have a concussion," I say, gently examining the wound. "We need to get you to a hospital."

"Hulk first," she says stubbornly.

A bark echoes from above us. Somehow, Hulk has managed to follow me. He's at the top of the slope, pacing anxiously along the edge of the trail, his large frame silhouetted against the darkening sky.

"Hulk," Callie cries, putting her hand up. "It's okay, baby, stay there."

"Goddammit," I mutter. "I told him to stay."

Callie lets out a sound somewhere between a laugh and a sob. "He doesn't listen to anyone but me."

Fair enough. I can't say I'd stay away if Callie needed me either. "We need to move," I say. "That slope is too steep for you to climb with your ankle, even with my help. I'm going to have to carry you."

She looks doubtful. "What about your knee?"

My knee is the last thing I'm worried about.

I grunt. "I've carried heavier packs through rougher terrain with worse injury," I assure her, turning to crouch with my back to her. "Put your arms around my neck."

With some awkward maneuvering and a few pained gasps from Callie, I get her settled on my back, her legs wrapped around my waist as best she can manage with her swollen ankle. I adjust my grip under her thighs as I begin the difficult climb. Each step strains my knee, but I focus on placing my feet carefully, following the path I took down.

"Thank you," she says softly. Her tears dampen my neck as the weight of her trust settles on my shoulders. A fierce protectiveness surges through me, something primal and absolute.

The earth beneath my feet shifts unexpectedly and my training takes over as I bite through the shock in my knee. I lock my jaw and maneuver up the remaining slope. "Almost there," I grunt as we near the top where Hulk waits, his tail wagging tentatively despite his obvious discomfort. Callie tightens her hold around my neck.

When we reach the cliff's edge and settle on the other side, Hulk immediately presses his body against Callie, whining softly as he nuzzles her face. She wraps her arms around his neck, burying her tear and blood-streaked face in his fur.

"You brave, brave boy," she whispers, voice thick with emotion.

I give them a moment, throat tight as I watch their reunion. Then reality reasserts itself. We're losing daylight fast. "Let's get going," I say, eyeing the darkening sky.

Callie nods, wincing as she tries to stand. "I can probably hobble—"

"No," I cut her off. "I'm going to carry you, but differently this time."

Her brow furrows. "What do you mean?"

"I need you in front of me," I explain, positioning myself before her. "Arms around my neck, legs around my waist."

Her cheeks flush slightly. "That's…"

"Practical," I counter. "We're heading downhill now. If I slip, I can fall backward and cushion you. And I need my arms free to grab onto trees or rocks if necessary."

Hesitantly, she reaches her arms out to me.

I crouch down, supporting her weight as she wraps her legs around my waist, careful of her ankle. "I got you," I mutter as I carefully lift her into my arms. For a moment, I'm struck by how perfectly she fits against me. Solid. Real. Her head naturally finds the hollow of my shoulder, her breath warm against my neck.

I've thought about holding her before, I realize. To have those wild, honey curls brush against my skin, to feel the rhythm of her heartbeat close to mine. The reality is more powerful than I could have imagined, even amidst the fear and urgency of the moment. One of her hands curls into the fabric of my shirt, her nails biting into my upper back.

"You okay?" I ask, securing my hands under her thighs.

She nods against my shoulder, her face close to mine. Hulk watches us before limping ahead a few steps and looking back expectantly.

As darkness falls around us, I pick my way down the mountain trail with Callie held tight in my arms. The descent is slow and treacherous. The trail narrows in places, forcing me to sidestep carefully. The uneven terrain taxes my already strained knee. I focus on my footing, hyperaware of her warmth against my chest.

"How's your knee?" she murmurs after we've been walking for about twenty minutes.

"I'm fine."

"You're a terrible liar," she says, but there's no heat in it.

I grunt in acknowledgment, unable to find the right words. My knee hurts, sure, but I'm not about to tell her that.

Her safety is more important than any pain I could be in.

Ahead of us, Hulk continues his determined march, but his limp is becoming more pronounced. His pace has slowed considerably.

"He's hurting bad," Callie whispers, concern in her voice.

"He's running on pure adrenaline and devotion," I reply.

She falls silent at that, arms tightening around me.

By the time the trailhead comes into view, twilight has fallen in earnest. Hulk's pace has slowed to a painful crawl. Callie's muscles tremble from the strain of holding on.

"Almost there," I encourage them both.

Hulk collapses the moment we reach the small gravel parking area, his sides heaving with exhaustion. The adrenaline that's been carrying him is spent. He whimpers when Callie calls his name.

I carefully lower her to sit beside him on the ground. She strokes his head, murmuring words of comfort while tears stream down her face.

"My truck," I tell her, already backing away. "Will you be okay for two minutes?"

"Yes," she sniffles, not taking her eyes off Hulk. "We'll be right here."

I take off at a run. The faster I get the truck, the sooner I can get them both medical attention. The gravel road crunches under my boots as I push myself harder than I should.

When I pull up minutes later, I find Callie exactly where I left her, cradling Hulk's massive head in her lap. The Shepherd's eyes are half-closed, but his tail thumps weakly against the ground when he sees me.

"I'll get him in first," I say, opening the back door of my extended cab.

Together, we coax Hulk to stand. With careful maneuvering and a lot of gentle reassurance from Callie, I manage to lift him into the backseat. He collapses again, breathing heavily. I turn to Callie next, lifting her into the passenger seat. I close the door and jog around the front to the driver's side. The moment I'm seated, Callie says without hesitation, "Animal hospital."

I glance at her bloody temple. "Callie, you need—"

"Animal hospital," she repeats, her voice brooking no argument. "Hulk is hurt. I can wait."

I study her for a moment. The determined set of her jaw, the pain in her eyes that has nothing to do with her physical injuries. "Fine," I say, starting the engine.

In the rearview mirror, I catch sight of Hulk stretched across the backseat, his loyal gaze fixed on Callie even in his exhaustion. She reaches back between the seats to rest her hand on his flank. "Good boy," she whispers.

Ten.

Beau

WE ARRIVED AT WHITETAIL Animal Hospital roughly an hour ago, and Callie still refuses to leave until we hear something. When we got here, the technicians took Hulk back straight away for X-rays and quickly found a severe ligament tear in his left hind leg. They whisked him away for emergency surgery and we've been sitting here ever since.

"Callie," I try again, but she isn't having any of it.

"Stop, please," she snaps, her eyes red and swollen from crying. "I'm not going until I hear he's okay. We'll go, I promise. Just...not yet."

I lean forward, my hands clasped in front of me with a resigned sigh. After another fifteen minutes of dreaded silence and her refusing to get herself looked at, I opt for a different angle. "When I was shot, I had about a dozen men ready to haul me out of the line of fire." I shake my head at the memory. "Waylon and Billings were arguing over who was going to escort me back. Fuckin' idiots."

Her focus is momentarily diverted when she glances at my knee, then my face. "What happened?"

I sigh heavily, surprised I've opened this particular door. It's not a story I've shared since coming home to the States. "I was their team leader. Told them both to shut up and get back into position. We were pinned down, four hostiles still in play. Couldn't afford to lose two men just to get me to safety."

She's watching me now, her emotional pain temporarily pushed aside by curiosity. "So what did you do?"

"Applied my tourniquet. Kept firing." I shrug. "I made them leave me there."

Her eyes widen. "By yourself? With a gunshot wound?"

"For about forty-five minutes. Until the area was secure."

"That's...insane."

"That's what the medic said, too." I cock a half grin. "By the time I let them haul me out of there, I'd lost a dangerous amount of blood. The bullet had fragmented and traveled, done a real number on my knee. If they'd evacuated me right away, like protocol dictated, the damage might not have been significant enough to warrant a discharge."

Understanding dawns in her eyes. "But you refused."

"I was a career soldier. I thought I was making the right call," I grunt. "Turns out, I was just being stubborn and ended up awarded a medical retirement at thirty-three."

"I'm sorry," she whispers.

"Don't be. It was a lesson I needed to learn." I meet her gaze. "Sometimes the bravest thing isn't pushing through the pain or refusing to leave your post. Sometimes it's admitting you need help, too."

She looks away, fresh tears welling in her eyes.

"He is in the best hands possible, Callie," I say softly, gesturing to her temple where dried blood still cakes her hairline. "You, on the other hand, need stitches. And that ankle needs to be properly examined."

"But what if..." Her voice breaks. "What if something happens while I'm gone? What if he needs me and I'm not here?"

"Dr. Mason promised to call the second there's any news," I remind her gently. "And Hulk's going to be in recovery for hours. He wouldn't want you sitting here suffering, would he?"

That gets her. She closes her eyes briefly. "No. He wouldn't."

"Let me take you to get patched up. For Hulk."

"Okay," she agrees, finally allowing me to help her to her feet.

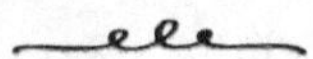

It's nearly midnight when we return to the animal hospital. Callie has three neat stitches at her temple, a walking boot on her moderately sprained ankle, and a prescription for mild painkillers that she'll have to fill in the morning.

"Miss Ryan," Dr. Mason greets us when we enter, her surgical cap still on. "Perfect timing. We've just moved Hulk to recovery."

"How is he?" Callie asks, breathless.

"The surgery went very well. Complete tear of the cranial cruciate ligament—what we'd call an ACL tear in humans. We performed a TPLO procedure." At Callie's confused expression, she explains, "We changed the angle of the top of his tibia so he doesn't need the ligament for stability anymore. It's the gold standard for large, active dogs like your Hulk."

Callie blows out a shaky breath. "Can I see him?" she asks, already moving toward the treatment area.

Dr. Mason nods. "Briefly. He's still coming out of anesthesia."

I hang back to give them privacy as the vet leads Callie through the double doors. When they return fifteen minutes later, Callie's eyes are red, but her expression is more at ease. "He recognized me," she tells me as she sits beside me in the waiting area. "He wagged his tail a little when he saw me."

I extend my arm behind her chair and she leans into me, taking the gesture as an open invitation. It wasn't, but I'll take it. "He's a fighter. You have nothing to worry about."

Dr. Mason returns to review the aftercare instructions with us. Strict rest for eight weeks, physical therapy, pain management. "He can go home tomorrow afternoon if all goes well tonight."

Callie's hand finds my thigh, and I fight my body not to react when her nails bite through my jeans. Her rapt gaze is on the good doctor.

"We'll keep him comfortable tonight and give you a call around noon tomorrow with a pickup time," she continues. "You should both go home and get some rest."

Callie is dead silent as the vet gives her a kind smile and retreats to the back room once again. I stand and offer her my hand. She stares at it for an unblinking moment before gently placing her hand in mine. I help her into my truck, her steps awkward in the new boot she's sporting. I close the passenger door and head to the driver's side.

The ride to the cabin is silent, aside from Callie's quiet sniffles. I should say something, reassure her that he's okay and he'll be home tomorrow, but I don't.

When I finally pull in the driveway and park, killing the engine, it's after one in the morning. I try like hell to find the right words to say and come up with, "Is there...anything I can do?"

Not bad. Could've been worse.

She breaks off into another fit of sobs, and my heart feels like it's being ripped out of my chest.

All right. Maybe I could've done better there.

"Hulk isn't just a PTSD service dog," she confesses, taking a deep breath in an attempt to calm herself. "He's a fully trained police attack dog that my father pushed through certification for me a few years ago to keep as a...a guard dog, more or less."

"A guard dog," I repeat, brow furrowed.

What the hell would she need a guard dog for?

"Hulk," she starts again, her voice shaking. "He watches my back so I'm not overwhelmed by this—this paranoid anxiety I have that somehow, no matter where I am, someone wants to hurt me. When I started taking Hulk everywhere with me, that feeling didn't stop right away, but it slowed. Little things that would send me into a spiral before didn't have the same effect. I felt lighter. He's been my backup for the last five years."

I stay silent as she speaks, taking in everything she's willing to give me.

"He's all I have. He's been through everything with me," she sniffles. "I don't know what I'm supposed to do now. I don't even have a phone to call and check on him."

"What do you mean?"

"My phone," she gestures vaguely up the road toward the trail, "it was in my backpack. It must have fallen off my back during the fall. I didn't even think about it when I gave the vet my information. And now they'll call, and I won't answer because I can't."

"We'll go in the morning," I say. "Get you a new phone and swing by the hospital to check on him. I'll give the state park service a shout in the morning to let them know that trail needs to be closed. They may be able to recover your bag as well."

Callie's head falls back against the headrest with a sniffle. "I'm sorry I'm such a mess," she says, rolling her head to face me. "I haven't even thanked you."

"Don't apologize," I grunt, looking away from her sad eyes. Even in her current state, she's damn near captivating. Her presence alone is drawing me in, wanting to prolong this moment of simply sitting in my truck and talking.

"Where did you stay last night?"

Her question catches me off guard. My face heats ever so slightly. *I can tell you where I shouldn't have slept.* "Here," I admit. "The other rental is open tonight, though. So I'll be there." I tip my chin toward the larger of the two cabins just ahead.

"That's good," she says, nodding to herself as her gaze drifts to the cabin.

For a moment, we sit in silence, darkness wrapped around us. "Well," I finally say, clearing my throat. "Let's get you inside. I assume your keys were in your pack, too?"

She sighs. "Yeah."

I come around to her side and help her out, offering my arm for support as she hobbles toward her cabin. The walking boot makes a dull thud against the wooden steps as we climb them to the front door.

I unlock the door and step aside as it opens with a creak. "Do you need anything before I go?" I don't know why I ask, or keep hovering, but I do. I couldn't force my legs to move away if I tried.

She shakes her head. "No, I...should be fine."

She doesn't look fine with the way she stands awkwardly beside the door, her hand on the doorframe as she peers inside. She looks lost. Vulnerable in a way that tugs at something deep in my chest.

"I'll be right next door," I say casually, jerking my thumb over my shoulder. "If you need anything. Anything at all."

She nods, but doesn't look up.

"Even if it's just…" I hesitate, searching for the right words. "If you don't want to be alone tonight. The offer stands."

Her gaze lifts to mine, searching my face for something. Ulterior motives, probably. "If you need backup, that is," I continue, feeling a little self-conscious at the offer I've made. I step back, giving her space. "Try to get some rest, Callie."

I turn away and walk to my truck, drawing in a deep breath of crisp, night air. *What am I doing?* This isn't like me—offering to stay with a woman as protection, inserting myself into her life. But something about Callie has gotten under my skin. It's been there since the moment I saw her.

I grab my duffel from the backseat, telling myself I'm being practical, kind. She's injured, distressed, and without a phone. It would be irresponsible to leave her alone.

"Beau?"

Her voice stops me when I start toward the rental. I turn. She's standing in her doorway, one hand braced against the frame for support. "Did you mean it?" she asks, her voice small. "About staying?"

"I don't say things I don't mean."

She nods slightly as if confirming something to herself. "Would you—I mean, would you mind? I know it's asking a lot, but—"

"It's not." I'm already walking toward her.

Relief visibly washes over her. "Thank you."

My jaw tightens at the hopeful expression she sends me as I approach. She opens the door farther. An invitation that has my pulse racing.

Be her backup. Nothing more.

"I really appreciate you doing this," she says quietly, closing the door behind me. I kick off my boots at the door. "I just... I don't think I can be alone with my thoughts right now."

I know all about the thoughts that come when there's nothing else to drown them out.

"And it's not like you haven't made yourself at home here before," she quips.

I freeze, glancing at her out of the corner of my eye.

"Sorry," she says, quick to apologize. A blush rises to her cheeks. "I didn't mean it like you weren't welcome. Well, I mean, you *weren't*, but now you *are*. I should probably stop talking."

Embarrassment creeps in. "Mind if I use the shower first?" I ask, needing to change the subject.

She nods, telling me to go ahead.

I close the bathroom door behind me and drop my bag on the floor before turning my gaze to the man in the mirror. Something shifted the moment I saw Hulk limping toward me, the determination in every painful step he took. The moment

I carried Callie down that mountain, her arms wrapped around my neck, trusting me completely despite barely knowing me aside from being her dick of a landlord who hates flowers and porch swings.

You've made one hell of an impression on her.

This is my chance to make things right.

Whatever this night is about to become, it certainly doesn't feel like there will be *nothing more* after tonight.

Eleven.

Callie

Well, this isn't codependent at all.

The moment Beau made the offer to be my 'backup' for the night in place of Hulk, I'd never wanted to accept someone's help so fast in my life. Telling him the truth about Hulk and what he means to me wasn't about gaining sympathy, it was about... Well, I'm not sure. After his confession, or story rather, from when he was shot, I felt like I needed to return the favor.

Silly, I suppose.

I should be anxious beyond measure with him in my house, using my bathroom, agreeing to sleep on the couch—be here alone with me all night. Instead, I'm calm for the first time in days.

I move around the small kitchen, fishing out my chamomile tea in hopes of calming my nerves enough to get some sleep tonight.

Hulk is going to need all my attention tomorrow. I fill the kettle and set it on the stove. The sound of the shower running provides a strangely domestic backdrop to my movements and feels far more natural than it should.

Beau Montgomery.

Former military, grumpy landlord, mountain rescue extraordinaire.

And now my temporary backup for the night.

The kettle whistles just as the water shuts off in the bathroom. I pour the boiling water over two tea bags, the fragrant steam rising to my face. My temple throbs with a heartbeat of its own, a steady reminder of today's events.

The bathroom door opens, and Beau emerges in a cloud of steam, wearing loose, black shorts and...nothing else. His hair is damp, random beads of water still clinging to his exposed chest and abdomen. He looks younger somehow, the day's grime finally washed away.

"I made tea," I say, holding up a mug.

His strong brow furrows as he drops his bag by the couch before walking toward me. "I don't think I've had tea before." He accepts the mug, our fingers brushing momentarily.

"Really?" I ask, surprised. "I buy this at the farmer's market on Tuesdays in town. There's a girl who grows and bags it all herself. You probably know her. I think she grew up here. Super sweet."

He grunts, sniffing the mug before tentatively bringing it to his lips. "Not bad." He lifts his chin toward me. "How's the head?"

"Hurts," I admit, propping a hip against the counter, my mug clasped between my hands as I blow on it softly.

He nods, taking another sip of his tea.

An awkward silence settles between us. We're somewhat strangers who've gone through an intense evening together, and now we're standing in my home drinking tea like old friends.

I'm not sure how to feel about it.

"I should probably shower, too," I say, setting my mug down. "Wash off all the..." I gesture vaguely to my blood and dirt-matted hair.

He steps back, giving me space as I walk past him. "If you need any help—" He stops abruptly and I lift my gaze in time to watch color rise to his cheeks. "I mean, with the walking boot, or—" He shakes his head. "Never mind. That came out wrong."

I can't help the small smile that crosses my face. Why does he seem so nervous? "I think I can manage."

I head for the bathroom, breathing in the lingering scent of his soap. The hot water is heaven on my sore muscles, though I have to be careful around my stitches and keep my weight on one foot. When I emerge fifteen minutes later, I'm wearing the only clean clothes I have left—silky sleep shorts and an oversized university hoodie. I've managed to get the walking boot back on, and suffice to say, it looks ridiculous paired with my pajamas.

Beau is sitting on the couch, his attention snapping to me when I limp into the room. His jaw ticks openly as he looks me over, then averts his gaze. "Better?" he asks, his voice rougher than before.

"Much." I lower myself carefully onto the opposite end of the couch, wincing as I prop my booted foot on the coffee table. "Though I'll feel a hundred percent better when I have Hulk back."

He watches me over the rim of his mug. "He's in good hands."

I snort a short laugh. "You keep saying that."

A slow grin loosens his hard features and the sight of it feels like a small victory compared to our first encounter. "Sorry. I'm not the best when it comes to comforting someone," he tells me. "Or with words."

I smile. "I think you're doing all right so far."

I peer over my shoulder at my tea I left on the counter in the kitchen, and without a word, he stands to retrieve it. When he hands it to me, I giggle. "See. You're already doing so good."

He smiles a second time as he retakes his seat beside me. "You're not gonna tell me I'm being a good boy, are you?"

I sputter with laughter, having to wipe tea from my lips while I eye him. Did he just make a joke? And a rather good one at that. "I can if you want me to," I tease.

He chuckles. "I think I'm all right."

We sit in silence for a moment, sipping from our mugs. It's not as awkward now. More contemplative on the day's events. I almost wish the couch was smaller so he'd sit closer. *Almost.*

"So," he says finally, "is there a boyfriend I should know about? Anyone who might show up I should be looking out for?"

The question catches me off guard. "No, um, no one and no boyfriend either." I tilt my head, studying him and the relaxation in his shoulders when I say, 'no boyfriend.' I shift in my spot, angling my body in a way my booted foot can rest on the cushion between us. My back to the arm of the couch to face him. "Why do you ask?"

He shrugs, refusing to meet my gaze. "Thought maybe there was someone who should know you're okay."

"My dad, maybe," I say, feeling a pang of worry at not having my phone to call him or Shea and tell them what happened. I curl my good leg beneath me. "What about you? Will your girlfriend be worried about you spending the night in another woman's cabin?"

The corner of his mouth quirks up. "No girlfriend."

Can't say I didn't pick up on that. "Interesting."

"Is it?" he asks far too quickly, but his dark eyes are on me now. I prefer them that way. *On me.*

I smile, the day's tension easing. "By the way," I start, tapping the ceramic mug with a fingernail. "And this is just to be clear, you know, set the record straight."

His brow furrows.

"It was the trail that caused us to fall, *not* my shoes."

One manly, judgy brow of his quirks upward. "If you say so," he mutters, lifting his mug to his lips smeared with a knowing grin. The jerk.

Though, I *will* be ordering hiking boots once my ankle heals.

I roll my eyes and change the subject. "So, tell me something I don't already know about you," I say, settling deeper into the couch.

"Not much to tell," he grumbles. "What you see is what you get."

"You're easier to read than you think, soldier boy."

His jaw ticks. "What's that supposed to mean?"

I shrug. "Nothing."

"If you've got something to say, say it." His tone is rough, defensive. And I fear I'm striking a nerve I didn't intend to.

"You can play tough guy all you like, but...I see you. I see what you want people to see, and I understand what you don't want them to see."

He's silent as he stares at me. His jaw ticks in time with what I assume are his racing thoughts. He looks away, and the moment slowly dies between us.

No one likes to be called out, but I think he may hate it the most.

"Come on," I coax, tapping his thigh with my booted foot in an attempt to lighten the mood. "There has to be something the world doesn't know about Beau Montgomery."

He scoffs, but seems to think for a moment. "I enjoy traveling," he says finally, and if I could do a tiny victory dance at him opening up with three words, I'd happily make a fool of myself. "Seeing new places, trying new foods. Not really a people person, though, so the two kind of clash a bit."

"Really?" I feign surprise. "Beau Montgomery isn't a people person? I'm shocked." I try to picture him standing outside the Eiffel Tower or viewing the Grand Canyon, those large arms crossed in front of him as he does. Silent. Stoic. Simply admiring the view. It fits, somehow.

He chuckles—*finally* letting loose. "Your turn."

"I write screenplays. Horror movies, to be specific."

His brows rise. "You're kidding."

"Have you ever seen *The Devil's Lake*?" I ask, and he nods. I point to myself. "All me."

"Now I'm impressed." He leans back, regarding me with new interest. "How did you get into that?"

The tea cools in my hands as I explain my writing journey throughout high school and college. He listens intently, asking questions here and there. The conversation flows easily from movies to places we've traveled and places we still wish to see someday.

It's strange how comfortable it feels, sitting here with him. Like we've known each other longer than a few weeks. Or maybe it's just him. Something about his steady presence makes me feel safe.

As I listen to him talk about his time overseas, I realize for the first time since the accident, I've gone several minutes without thinking about Hulk. The guilt is immediate, but then I remember what Beau said earlier about how *sometimes the bravest thing is accepting help*, and the tension in my shoulders eases.

Maybe, just for tonight, I can let myself be distracted by this unexpected friendship.

Hulk would approve, I think.

Twelve.

Beau

The bachelor party group chat that Rhett decided to throw me into goes off three times in quick succession. I grit my teeth in response. I was supposed to meet everyone at the bar an hour ago, but Callie texted me not too long ago asking if I could help her get Hulk down from her Jeep when she gets home.

And like hell was I going to say no.

Last night felt...right. She fell asleep on the couch while we talked. Her feet had somehow ended up in my lap, and I wasn't about to wake her to move. Instead, I tossed the throw blanket over us and sat there all night. I dozed off a bit, but woke anytime she moved to get comfortable. She apologized half a dozen times when she finally did wake. And I wished she hadn't.

There was nothing to be sorry for.

She made us breakfast, and we talked about our plans for the day. Hers included running to the store for a new phone and stopping by the animal hospital to check on Hulk. I offered to go with her because, truth be told, I need to take it easy today. There's some swelling in my knee from yesterday's exertion, and I'm not trying to push my luck any further than I already have.

Unfortunately, she declined my offer, thinking I had work to do on the new cabin build before I needed to get ready for my brothers' dual bachelor party tonight.

Then, as I was about to leave for the bar, she texted me, asking for help.

I must look like one hell of a sucker sitting here waiting on her as friends of my new sisters-in-law begin showing up for the bachelorette party they're throwing at the rental cabin.

I can't stand the side eyes of curiosity much longer.

Less than a minute later, however, Callie's Jeep pulls in. Slow and steady. I stand, not seeing Hulk in the front seat as I have in the past. I walk toward her as she kills the engine and hops out onto her booted foot with a cringe.

"Hey, sorry we're late," she says, limping to the trunk of the car. "I didn't want to go too fast and jostle him. I even took the long way around town to avoid the mass of potholes on Main."

"No worries," I say, popping the tailgate open to a big, cone-headed pup. "How is he?"

"A little high, I think." She giggles, the sound melodic enough to draw me a step closer. "They had a heck of a time managing his pain meds throughout the night, I guess. So he's still coming down from some strong stuff."

"Did you fill your script?" I ask, maneuvering Hulk in a way I can hook my arms under him to lift him. His ears perk to greet me, his tongue lolling out of his mouth. He looks happy to see me. *Definitely high.*

"Yes," she says, hurrying beside me to catch the blanket he was lying on.

I slow my steps to keep her from straining her ankle. She's moving with more confidence than yesterday, but clearly favoring her right.

Hulk's considerable weight is solid in my arms, and I'm reminded again of how big he truly is. The German Shepherd seems content being carried, though his head rests trustingly against my shoulder.

Callie opens the door and I step carefully into the cabin, following her directions as she gestures toward the back door. "I set up his bed over by the patio door," she explains. "I figured it would be easier for him to go out that way. Less walking."

I gently lower Hulk onto the plush dog bed. Pillows, blankets, toys. His food and water bowls are close by. He settles with a contented sigh, stretching out his front paws. The plastic cone around his neck bumps against the floor, and he gives me a look of such dignified resignation that I can't help but smile.

"Home sweet home," I say, giving his head a gentle scratch.

Callie kneels beside him, running her fingers through his fur, careful to avoid his bandaged back leg. "Thank you for waiting," she says, looking at me in a way that does something to my chest. "And you'll..." She hesitates, her hand resting on Hulk. "Will you be coming back tonight? After?"

The question hangs between us, loaded with implications I'm not sure either of us are ready to address. Part of me wants to say yes immediately—the part that's drawn to her presence, her gaze, her attention. While another part recognizes how this temporary arrangement could complicate things.

I'm her landlord, after all.

"Do you want me to?" I ask.

She meets my gaze and something vulnerable flickers across her face. "I just thought—"

My phone rings in my pocket, cutting the conversation short. When I glance at the screen, I see Rhett's name.

"You're late," she says softly. "You should go."

I hesitate, looking at Hulk splayed out on his bed, then back to Callie. "Are you sure?"

It certainly wouldn't ruin my night to stay in with her over partying with my brothers and their rowdy group. I don't tell her that, though. For some reason, I have this asinine need to hear her ask me to stay.

"We'll be fine. You've already done more than enough."

"I'll text you," I say, reluctant to leave. "To check in."

"I'd like that."

At the door, I turn back for one last look. Callie has settled herself on the floor next to Hulk, her injured leg stretched out in front of her, one hand stroking his fur.

"Have fun tonight," she calls.

I glance over my shoulder and note she never explicitly told me not to come back. The unspoken invitation follows me out the door and stays with me as I drive into town.

I park my truck outside of Tavern Nine and opt to sit in silence for a moment before I'm thrust into a brother-bonding experience I didn't consent to. My mind continues to replay the look on Callie's face when she asked if I'd be coming back.

What did she mean? To stay? To spend the night again?

Or was it a friendly 'hangout' invitation?

My head floods with thoughts as the lot continues to fill with vehicles. I walk toward the front of the bar. The heavy wooden door swings open, releasing a wave of noise alongside the scent of fried food and alcohol. Country music drowns out most conversation, but I spot my brothers and a few others near the pool tables off the back of the bar.

I was told the new 'pool room' here is a recent addition built by Rhett and Levi's construction company, and Roger, the owner, reserved it specially for our group tonight at no charge.

"There he is!" Rhett's voice booms over the music when he spots me heading their way.

Butch raises his beer in my direction, his smile wide beneath his thick beard. Levi, our youngest brother, is already three sheets to the wind, judging by his flushed face and the horrible shot he just took at the table. "Son of a—"

"Thought you might bail," Rhett says, clapping my shoulder as I approach.

"Considered it," I reply, accepting the beer Duke passes my way. I'm not a big drinker, never have been, but tonight... I wouldn't mind the distraction.

"Rough night in the tent?" Duke asks with a knowing smirk. He lives right up the road. No doubt he saw the state of it the other day on his way to work.

"Tent's history."

"So, where you been crashing?" Levi slurs, throwing an arm around my shoulders as Stan, Butch's best friend, takes his shot at the eightball and sinks it. Levi huffs.

The memory of Callie's face when she found me on her couch flashes in my mind. Then her sound asleep beside me all night and into the morning. "Truck," I lie, taking a swig of my beer.

Rhett raises a brow but doesn't get a chance to press the issue as a waitress arrives with ten shots. We each take a glass. "To the futures of the current Mr. and Mrs. Butch Montgomery *and* Mr. and Mrs. Duke Montgomery," Rhett hoots, reminding me that even though this is a bachelor party for my brothers, they're both already married. The wedding reception was simply postponed for whatever reason. Babies, I suppose.

Everyone cheers, takes their shot, and returns to the informal pool competition. I force myself to join in—it's what I'm supposed to do. These are my brothers, my family. This is home.

So why do I feel like I belong somewhere else entirely?

A few hours later, and one too many beers, Rhett takes the stool beside mine. "You gonna tell me what happened with the pretty neighbor, or am I gonna have to guess?"

I stare straight ahead, jaw tight. "Nothing to tell."

"That bad, huh?" He chuckles. "Well, the night is young, brother. Plenty of distractions here."

As if on cue, a group of women enter the bar, drawing appreciative glances from the single men in our crowd. I keep my gaze averted and grip my beer tightly. A lame attempt to focus on the celebration, on anything but the jump in my leg that's urging me to leave and get the answer to the one question that's plaguing my mind: *Does she feel the same pull I do?*

What the hell is wrong with me? I sound like a fucking sad sap, pining over some chick.

"What's on your mind?" Rhett asks, pulling me from my thoughts as he takes the high-top seat beside me.

I shake my head and busy myself with a swig of beer. "Nothing."

"Doesn't seem like nothin'. You've got that same look you had when Tracy Wilks started flirting with Duke back in grade school. There's something on your mind. Spit it out."

I wouldn't normally ask one of my brothers for dating advice, but out of all of them, I know I can talk to Rhett without fear of judgment. And after three beers and two shots, I may convince myself it's a good idea. "Do you think I'm...easy to read?"

Rhett tips his beer from side to side, eyeing me curiously. "Why do you ask?"

I cross my arms and lean against the back of my chair. "Callie said—"

"Ohhh, I see." My brother chuckles. "Lady troubles?"

I huff. "Not really a trouble."

"It's like that, huh?" He smiles, gesturing as if telling me to continue. "Go on. Let's hear the details of how fucked you are for this girl."

My scoff turns to laughter at the truth behind the statement. I tell him the truth about where I slept last night—avoiding the breaking and entering a few nights prior—and why I was late tonight.

Rhett shakes his head. "Dating is...fucking hard, man," he says, drinking the last of his beer. "It's not the same. There are apps and services and social media. You walk up to a girl at a gas station to hit on her and she thinks she's about to be kidnapped."

"Amen to that," Levi chimes in, staggering over to the table. "It's a war zone out there, bro. A war we ain't gonna win."

Rhett rolls his eyes. "Shut up, man. Just because you keep getting shot down for the long term doesn't mean Beau doesn't have a chance."

Levi snarls at our brother.

"I get it," I say, interrupting whatever bickering match they're about to start on.

"Ah, ah, ah!" Stan whistles, catching the group's attention. He points between Butch and Duke who are simultaneously on their phones and texting. "No checking on wives during bro night."

"The girls need more tequila," Butch says, his gaze shifting to Duke. "Cassidy asked if we could swing by the cabin on our way back."

Duke nods. "Maci forgot her breast pump. You ready now?"

"Cabin?" Stan asks, interrupting their conversation.

"The girls decided to do a bachelorette party at Beau's rental," Duke tells him.

"Alison says it's not a real bachelorette if there aren't strippers, so it's just a girls' night," Tanner, another one of Butch's friends, chimes in.

Butch glares at him. "There better not be any strippers showing up."

Rhett claps me on the shoulder. "You know, Cassidy mentioned something about inviting Callie."

My beer freezes halfway to my lips. "She invited Callie?" Then there *really* better not be any fucking male strippers over there.

Butch scrolls through his phone. "Yeah, Cass says she knocked on her door earlier but got no answer."

Irrational worry slices through me. *She's probably just busy taking care of Hulk.*

The guys agree to the impromptu supply run for the girls, and I find myself at the head of the pack. A part of me is saying, *I need to see her.*

If my brothers are right, then I'm heading straight into a war zone.

And I'd gladly walk into war for her.

Thirteen.

Callie

"But you're okay? And Hulk, he's okay, too?" Shea asks for the second time.

I hold the phone pinned between my cheek and shoulder as I shuffle to Hulk's bed, fresh water and his packed food bowls in hand. "We're okay," I reply. "I'm giving him his dinner now and nightly pain meds shortly. He'll be zonked out within the hour."

"Jesus, Cals," she breathes. "You can't scare me like that. I almost called your dad."

I snort, recalling the phone conversation I had with him shortly before I called her. Long story short, it was an earful. "I'm glad you didn't. He probably would've shown up here."

"Can you blame him?"

I sit on the floor beside Hulk, removing his cone so he can eat. "I guess not."

"She guesses not," Shea scoffs on the other end of the phone. "Thank god Brian was there to help you."

"Beau." I laugh. "His name is *Beau*. And don't act like you don't remember. Call him nice-chest-guy if you must."

She snickers. "I was hoping you'd catch that," she says. "So, explain to me what happened after he took you home."

I nod, even though she can't see me. "He offered to stay the night so I wasn't alone." At the sound of her squeal, I add, "Nothing happened. We just talked and he kept my mind off everything, really."

"And?" she coaxes.

"And it was...nice." I don't elaborate or tell her how he asked if I had a boyfriend, doted on me, and even rubbed my feet when the boot started to pinch my leg.

"Hmm. I'm going to need more context here. Where did he sleep?"

I scrunch my nose. "The couch."

"And you were..."

"Also, on the couch."

"I knew it!" she sings, laughing in delight. "Oh, my god. I *cannot* wait to meet this guy. We'll have to plan something, the three of us. What time do you fly in again? I'll need to meet you—"

"Wait, huh?" My brow furrows, confused. "What are you talking about?"

"The premiere," she says. "He did say he'd come with you, didn't he?"

I don't follow. "Why would he come to the—" I gasp, realization dawning on me as my gaze snaps to Hulk's. "Oh, no." I fly in for the premiere in only three weeks. Hulk won't be able to travel in that short of time. He needs to rest and heal. Which means he won't be able to go with me to LA.

I'll be without him for *two whole weeks.*

"I thought that's what you were talking about," she says. "Why don't you ask him? I doubt he'd say no. I mean, have you *seen* yourself? And you said he offered in the first place."

"Yeah, but..." My eyes begin to water at the very idea of having to leave Hulk. I was without him for one night and it was awful. Well, not *awful* with Beau around, but I missed him like crazy.

"You can't miss the premiere. It's the final chapter."

"I know," I mutter, biting my fingernail in thought. Could I ask Beau? Would he come with me? The guy offered *one* night, not weeks of his time. "I don't know, Shea. He always seems so busy."

"Then pay the guy. You said he doesn't have a job, so why not this? I mean, be honest, if Beau doesn't come with you, what would plan B be?"

"This wasn't even plan A," I huff.

"Plan C, then. You know what I mean."

I do know what she means, and I also know the point she's trying to make. I sigh. "I'd hire a bodyguard."

"Exactly. You would hire someone to attend all the events with you and be your two-legged version of Hulk," she states proudly. "You already have security meeting you at the interviews and events, why not ask Beau to attend everything with you? And...he can get your bestie's stamp of approval at the same time."

I smile. "A very important stamp."

"A *very* important stamp, ma'am."

"This whole side conversation is pointless. I don't even know if I like him like that..." I trail off, hearing the lie in my voice at the same time Shea does.

"You like him enough to trust him," she says, softer now. "Isn't that enough for now?"

A light knock on my front door has me jumping in my spot perched on the floor. Hulk perks up beside me and looks at me, waiting for my reaction.

"I have to go. Someone's here."

"Ooh! Is that him? Okay, okay. Text me later. Love you."

I roll my eyes and laugh. "Love you, too." I hang up the phone and get to my feet. When I reach the window beside the door, brushing the curtain aside to peer out and see who it is, I'm surprised to find Cassidy walking away. Six cars lining the driveway catch my attention at the same time.

I wonder what's going on next door? I haven't spent much time with her, usually only seeing her in passing with Maci and their babies at the store or around town. I chew my lower lip, debating whether to let her walk away or open the door.

Hulk's whine decides it. I return to his side a moment later, and he bumps my hand, telling me he needs to be let out to do his business.

"Okay, big boy. Just like before." I grab the towel I've been using to help support his hind legs and slide it under him, hoisting his rear in the air as we slowly make our way out the patio door and onto the back porch. It takes him a moment to get down the two short steps, but he manages.

Once he's done, we make our way back up to the porch when he stops by the fire pit. He lies down with his front paws, forcing me to ease his booty down, too.

"Really?" I sigh as he peers up at me with puppy eyes, making me feel like some villain for straying away from our routine. "You're lucky you're so darn cute," I mutter. "Let me get your other blanket. I don't want you getting dirty."

I hurry inside to get him a blanket to lie on and get him settled before fetching a few pieces of firewood from my little stockpile. I'm busy lighting a match when loud laughter and shouting next door catches my attention.

I glance over my shoulder and Hulk's ears perk up. They must be having a party. Is that why Cassidy stopped by earlier? To let me know they'd be a bit loud tonight? I suppose that makes sense.

I pull my outdoor chair close to Hulk's spot by the fire that's steadily growing. "We won't stay out too long," I tell him, petting his head and toying with his ears.

The fire crackles, sending sparks up into the night sky. Hulk rests his head on his paws, his eyes drooping as he enjoys the warmth.

The sliding glass door next door squeaks open, and I glance over to see Maci stepping onto the back porch. A pudgy dachshund waddles out beside her, his little legs barely keeping his belly from dragging on the ground.

"Come on, Frankie. Do your business," she says, wrapping her cardigan tighter around herself. She notices our fire and does a double-take, surprised to see me. "Callie? Is that you?"

I give her a small wave. "Hey, Maci."

She hesitates for a moment before calling over, "Mind if I join you while this little guy takes his sweet time?"

I laugh. "Not at all."

Maci waits for Frankie to sniff around the edge of the porch before making her way over to our fire. She's careful not to trip over any roots or stones in the dark, her steps illuminated by the flickering firelight.

"Cassidy stopped by earlier," she says, warming her hands over the fire. "She said you weren't home." Maci glances over at Hulk, who's watching her with gentle eyes. "What happened? You both look pretty banged up."

I gesture vaguely up the mountain. "Took a tumble off one of the hiking trails."

She gapes. "Oh, no."

I shake my head. "Yeah, it wasn't fun. But we're okay."

"Good." She nods as Frankie hobbles over to us.

When he spots Hulk, his whole body begins to wiggle in excitement at seeing his much bigger buddy. He heads in our direction. I've met Frankie a few times—once when Cassidy came to help Mrs. Montgomery clean the rental cabin after a large family left a huge mess, and recently when Butch was over helping Beau cut down a few trees a few weeks ago. Hulk and Frankie have become fast friends. I feel a bit guilty he can't play with his short friend.

They're hilarious to watch play together, given their size difference.

Frankie sniffs Hulk's wrapped hind leg and whines softly before picking a spot on his blanket and having a seat. We sit in comfortable silence for a moment, watching the flames dance.

I lift my chin toward the music coming from the rental cabin. "Having a party?"

"Yeah. It's just a little bachelorette get-together for Cassidy and me." Maci yawns. "Nothing wild."

"Moms' night out." I smile faintly, and Maci yawns a second time. "How come you're not inside partying with the rest of them?"

She shrugs, then checks her phone before peering up at me. "Not a big particr," she says. "Or drinker. I'm more of a babysitter for tonight. This is Cassidy's first night out in almost two years."

"Oh, boy."

Maci laughs. "Exactly. But don't let her fool you, she was crying for the first hour after we dropped the babies off with Duke's mom."

"How is Olivia doing?"

"She's amazing," Maci beams, swiping on her phone to show me a picture of her daughter and Cassidy and Butch's son playing. "Julie is watching her and Gage for the night. It's her first time with both babies at once. She went a bit...over the top with toy purchases for the house."

I smile as she swipes through the dozens of pictures Julie sent of the babies surrounded by toys. My heart melts at how lucky they are to have such a wonderful, hands-on grandmother.

The sound of laughter gets louder, and the back door slides open again. A woman's voice calls out, "Maci? Everything okay?"

"I'm over here," she calls back with a wave of her hand.

"You started a fire without us?" Seconds later, Cassidy appears at the edge of the yard, slightly unsteady on her feet. She's holding a wine glass that sloshes dangerously as she walks. Behind her, three other women follow, each carrying drinks.

"Callie!" Cassidy exclaims when she sees me. "I stopped by earlier. I wanted to invite you to join us."

"Sorry about that," I say, awkward at seeing her so intoxicated. We've only met a handful of times.

"Well, now we're bringing the party to you," she announces, throwing her arms wide and nearly spilling her glass. "Bonfire time!"

I glance at Hulk, who's watching the newcomers with mild interest, his tail giving a single weak thump against his blanket. This definitely wasn't what I had planned for our quiet evening in.

Not really having much choice, the group of women are already arranging themselves around the fire pit. A few fetch chairs from their cars while others grab dining chairs from the cabin.

One of the women, a stout blonde I've never met, looks around. "We need marshmallows. Do you have marshmallows, Callie?" she asks, adding as an afterthought, "I'm Alison, by the way. Cassidy's maid of honor." She gestures proudly to her sash.

Before I can answer, more women emerge from next door, carrying folding chairs and bottles of wine. "I found more chairs," one of them announces triumphantly.

Maci catches my eye and mouths *'sorry'* with an apologetic smile.

I take a deep breath and look down at Hulk, who seems surprisingly unbothered by all the commotion. His eyes meet mine, and I swear I can see a glint of amusement there, as if to say, *"Well, this is different."*

As the women settle in, chattering excitedly about playing *Cards Against Humanity* by the fire, I lean over to scratch behind Hulk's ears. Maybe this isn't what we planned, but sometimes life's interruptions are exactly what we need.

"Can I get you something to drink?" Maci asks. "We've got everything except tequila—we're running low."

"I'm okay, but thank you," I say, smiling at the little naked men sitting on the rim of everyone's drinks.

Conversation continues around me—laughter and stories, occasionally including me with a smile or question. An hour passes, and I'm much more relaxed, even laughing at some of their wedding planning disaster stories. Frankie sits at my feet, watching me eat a handful of pretzels someone brought out with big, greedy eyes.

"So, Callie," Alison asks, setting up a card game, "how do you like living out here in the middle of nowhere?"

"I love it," I answer honestly.

"And how's having Beau Montgomery as your landlord?" Cassidy asks curiously, pouring herself another glass of red. "I swear he came back with the personality of a grizzly bear."

Heat rushes to my cheeks as unwanted images flood my mind: Beau asleep with a towel draped low on his hips, his muscled chest rising and falling with each breath. Beau walking around my cabin shirtless. Beau fetching me tea and rubbing my feet. Beau smiling. Beau laughing. Beau carrying me and Hulk to safety like a true mountain man.

"We don't really...interact much," I say. *Liar, liar.*

Cassidy snorts, taking the five cards Alison hands her. "That's Beau for you. The Montgomery brother who's allergic to human interaction."

My brow furrows. "Why do you say that?"

"Callie," Beau says, his voice low and gravelly and draws my attention straight to him. A stern sort of glare directed at his brother.

"On that note." Rhett leaps to his feet with a grin, his elbow bumping Beau's as he walks toward the cabin. "Told you."

Beau huffs before returning his gaze to me. His hard exterior slips to something softer. He gestures to the spot Rhett just vacated. "You mind?"

I shake my head. "No, no. Sit."

The silence between us is both awkward and comforting at once.

"So, you, uh…" he starts, but doesn't finish.

I peer at him out of the corner of my eye and note the way his thumb picks at the label on his beer bottle. He looks tortured attempting to find the right words to say. It's almost cute how hard he's trying.

Okay, fine, it *is* cute.

Rhett calls out to a few of the girls still lingering by the fire and suddenly it's just me, Beau, and the dogs sleeping soundly beside the dying fire.

I decide to break the silence first. "How was the bar?"

"Good," he says with a slight nod. "How are you feeling?"

I bite my lip to keep from smiling at his concern. "Headache is gone. Ankle feels better. I might take the boot off tomorrow and see how I fare."

"Doctor said to keep it on for a week minimum."

I roll my eyes. "At my discretion."

His grin is slow and wide as he looks at me. "Stubborn."

I giggle. "You would know."

He laughs, his gaze dancing over me. The glow of the fire illuminating his face in a way that reveals every hard angle I've come to memorize. The flickering shadows play across his features, highlighting the small scar above his eyebrow and the slight curl at the corner of his mouth as he looks at me. "Hulk settling in okay?"

I shift my attention to the two sleeping boys beside us. "He's doing okay, I think. I actually need to bring him in soon and give him his pain meds for the night."

He nods, taking a swig of his beer as we fall into another amicable silence.

"Callie," he starts. "I want—"

A loud whistle catches us off guard as one of the men Beau came in with puts his hands in the air. "Let's go, kids! Bro night continues."

"Bro night?" I say, laughing lightly.

"Cigars and poker, apparently," Beau grumbles, pushing to stand with a bit more care on his left knee than I've seen from him.

The urge to ask him if he's feeling okay teeters on the tip of my tongue. Instead, I say, "Have fun."

He looks down at me. His eyes—a rich brown that reminds me of warm whiskey—hold mine with an intensity that makes my breath catch. The corner of his mouth twitches. Not quite a smile, but close.

"Yo, Beau, you coming or what?" Levi calls from the doorway, his words slightly slurred and only a third of the block of cheese remaining in his hand.

How the heck did he eat so much so fast?

"Yeah," Beau responds, not taking his eyes off me. "I'll see you in a few hours," he tells me, his voice dropping low in a way I'm not prepared for.

My heart skips in my chest and heat flashes between my thighs. *I will?* "Okay," I say, attempting lightness. "See you soon."

This time, his smile transforms his stern face into something handsome and...boyish. He'd probably be mortified if he knew I thought he was puppy-dog-cute over anything rugged and manly. He joins his brothers, leaving me with a strange flutter in my chest.

He passes Cassidy and her group of girlfriends returning to the fire with cups and a bottle of tequila. Maci nowhere in sight.

"Well, *that* was interesting," Lily says, dropping onto the chair opposite me with an eager expression.

Heat creeps up my neck. "What's that?"

"My brother doesn't look at people the way he was just looking at you." Lily takes a sip of her drink, eyes twinkling.

"Oh my *god*." Cassidy gasps, covering her mouth. "This explains why Butch was saying Beau's been even more broody than usual today."

I stand quickly and head for the woodpile to throw a few more pieces in the fire pit. "I don't know what you're getting at, but it's

not like that. He's my landlord and, like you said, he's an asshole."
Lies, lies, lies.

"I used to think Butch was an asshole once," Cassidy says wistfully. "Now we're married and I needed a c-section just to birth his big ass baby."

The women laugh and continue their night unbothered.

Meanwhile, I can't help wondering what Beau wanted to tell me before he was interrupted. And what time he'll be back tonight. The thought of seeing him again sends a flutter through my stomach. Whatever this is between us, it's becoming something I can't ignore.

Fourteen.

Beau

It's just after one in the morning when I catch a ride from Tanner back to my property.

To Callie.

I smell like Cuban cigars and whiskey, but overall, it was a good night. I'm not drunk—*I don't think*—and I certainly wasn't going to be driving myself home after the shots the guys were doling out an hour ago.

I stumble up the steps of her greenhouse of a front porch and dig in my pocket for my keys. It takes me a good three minutes to find them—in my front pocket, of course—and I realize I *may* be a bit tipsier than I thought.

The lock clicks quietly as I turn the key. I ease the door open, trying to keep the hinges from squeaking. The cabin is dark except for a small night light in the kitchen that casts just enough glow for me to see where I'm going. I slip off my boots by the door, leaving them beside Callie's sneakers.

Something about seeing our shoes side by side makes my chest tighten.

Must be the whiskey...

I need to piss like a racehorse after all those drinks, which means navigating through her bedroom to the bathroom. Great planning on my part to build a cabin with one bathroom only accessible through the bedroom. At the time, it made perfect sense—given this was meant to be *my* cabin when home.

Now, it's an exercise in stealth.

The door to her bedroom is cracked open. I push it gently, wincing at the soft creak it makes. Moonlight streams through the window, illuminating her form under the covers. Hulk is stretched out on his dog bed, dragged to the end of Callie's bed. His eyes gleam in the darkness, tracking my movement.

He doesn't bark or growl at me, though. *Progress.*

Callie is curled on her side, one arm tucked under her pillow, the other draped across where I should be. Her shoulder-length, honey-blonde hair is fanned out across the pillow. Her lips slightly parted. I stop for a moment, watching her breathe.

When did this woman start to matter so much to me?

I try to tiptoe across the worn hardwood floor, but a board creaks loudly under my weight. *Fuck*. She stirs, turning over slightly. I freeze, but she doesn't wake fully. Taking my chance, I slip into the bathroom as quietly as possible.

After using the bathroom and splashing some cold water on my face, I emerge to find her blinking sleepily in my direction.

"Beau?" Her voice is husky with sleep. "What time is it?"

"Late," I whisper. "Go back to sleep."

She props herself up on one elbow, hair falling over her shoulder. "You're home."

Something about the way she says 'home' makes my stomach flip. I swallow hard, wishing I'd brushed my teeth before coming out. "Yeah, I'm home."

"Did you have fun?" She's more awake now, eyes adjusting to the darkness.

"It was all right." I shrug, standing a few feet away from the bed. "The guys were in rare form tonight."

She smiles, and even in the dim light, it does something to me. "Is that why you smell like a distillery?"

I chuckle. "That obvious, huh?" I run a hand through my hair, feeling strangely self-conscious.

"Just a little." She pulls herself to a sitting position, the covers falling to her waist. She's wearing one of her loose, silky tank tops, a slim strap slipping off one shoulder. "Are you drunk, Beau?"

"Not drunk," I clarify, though the room does have a slight tilt to it. "Relaxed."

"Mmhm." She doesn't sound convinced. "You know what I think?"

"What's that?"

"I think you're trying *very* hard to look sober right now," she says, amusement in her voice rather than judgment.

I can't help but smile. "Maybe a little."

"Don't let me stop you." She gestures toward the open bedroom door, but as I start to move, she reaches out and catches my wrist. "Wait."

I stop, looking down at her hand on my skin. Cool to the touch, yet it ignites a fire deep inside me. "What's wrong?"

"Nothing." She tugs gently. "Will you...come here a second?"

I hesitate, then sit on the edge of the bed at her request. Hulk gives a soft snort from the foot of the bed, but doesn't move. Clearly, *he's* the one judging me tonight.

"I was worried," she says quietly. "You didn't text me back."

Guilt gnaws at me. I meant to, but the night got away from me. "I'm sorry. Things got rowdy and Stan was threatening to take away phones. I forgot."

She's quiet for a moment. Her eyes, soft in the moonlight, search my face. "Did you at least win some money?"

I chuckle. "Actually, yeah. About three hundred. If you think I'm a shit liar, you should've seen Duke. He quit after the second round."

She smiles softly. "I'm glad you had fun."

Her fingers are still around my wrist, her thumb absently stroking my pulse point. Does she know what she's doing to me? Can she feel my heart racing sitting beside her?

Something about the way she's looking at me makes everything slow down. Disappear. Refocus. *Fuckin' hell, she's beautiful.* "Callie..."

"You look good," she says out of fucking *nowhere*. Her gaze drops to my mouth. My cock thickens at the mere glance. "All rough and...you know."

I have no idea what she's talking about, but I can't stop staring at her. "Yeah?"

The air between us shifts, charged with whatever energy she's putting out. And whatever the hell it is, I'm drawn to it. A moth to her flame. *Only her.*

She nods, then sits up on her knees in an attempt to match my height beside the bed. Her hands dance up and down my forearms. Her touch is light, but it sends heat racing down my spine at the thought of her hands elsewhere.

"Yeah," she breathes.

"I should shower," I say, not moving an inch. "I smell like—"

"I don't mind," she cuts me off, her voice dropping lower. Seductive. "Not right now."

I may have been out of the dating game for many years now, and *fuck*...

It's been a long time since I've been with a woman.

My heart hammers against my ribs as she leans closer. I can smell the faint floral of her shampoo, see the flecks of gold in her eyes. Gorgeous. *You have no idea how bad I want you, sweetheart.*

"Callie," I say again, my voice rough from all the whiskey and smoke. I need to get my shit together. Figure out what's going through her head. Because if we do this... "What are we doing?"

She doesn't answer. She closes the distance between us, urging me to bend toward her as her lips meet mine hesitantly at first, then with growing need. My hands find her waist, pulling her flush against me as our kiss deepens. The soft gasp she makes sends heat racing through me.

Her arms circle my neck and her fingers thread through my hair, nails lightly scraping my scalp. I groan. Her lips are warm and pliant under mine. My tongue traces the seam of her lips and she opens for me. Our tongues meet in a slow, sensual dance. The whiskey on my breath mingles with her sweetness, creating an intoxicating flavor that's entirely us.

Whiskey and honey.

I've spent a second tasting her and I'm fucking addicted.

When we finally break apart, she's breathing hard, her cheeks flushed. "I've wanted to do that for a while now," she admits, her fingertips dancing over the back of my neck. "I got tired of waiting for you to make the first move."

My thumb traces the curve of her jaw, tilting her gaze to mine. I search her eyes, desperate to know. "You want me, sweetheart?" I ask. Low, tentative, like her answer might break me.

And it does.

At her shallow nod, I growl.

My cock hard and straining in my jeans, I kiss her again, slower this time, savoring the way she melts against me. My hand slides up her back, feeling the warmth of her skin under her thin top.

Her hands come to rest on my shoulders, then slide down my chest until she's gliding her fingers beneath my shirt. Her palms flat against my chest. "I've been thinking about you a lot lately," she says softly, her nails gliding over my pecs.

"Callie," I groan. I grip her hips firmly. Ready to hold her in place permanently, or end this all together. "Are you sure about this?"

She looks up at me through thick, knee-weakening lashes, and the sight nearly undoes me.

"Yes."

Goddammit.

I capture her mouth with mine. The kiss hungrier, deeper. Her body responds as she presses against me, her hands grasping at my shoulders for purchase as I lean over her.

"Lie down," I growl against her lips.

I gently lay her back onto the bed. Her hair fans over the pillow, and moonlight catches the flush spreading across her cheeks and down her neck. Her breath quickens.

I prowl over her on the bed, my knee resting between her thighs. I press my lips to her collarbone, neck, jaw, before trailing down her sternum. I take my time, and with every breath on her skin, she arches into me. I push her shirt up slowly, revealing every inch of honey-soft skin. She watches me, her breath coming faster as my fingers graze over the peaks of her breasts. I bend to kiss between them, over her heart.

"Beau," she whispers, her hands threading through my hair.

"Let me take care of you," I tell her, my lips moving to the soft curve of her breast.

She arches her back as I lick and suck at one pert nipple. She whimpers when I pull away to kiss down her stomach. My rough palms slide along her sides, memorizing every dip, every curve. When I reach the waistband of her shorts, I look up at her, seeking permission.

She lifts her hips and I slowly slide them down her legs. *No panties. No bra.*

She knew what she wanted tonight.

The sight of her, laid out before me in nothing but the dim light of the moon, steals my breath. "Fucking beautiful," I groan.

My cock strains painfully in my jeans as I position myself between her legs and gently part her thighs. The glisten of her pretty pink pussy has my cock weeping.

Her breathing grows ragged, and when I finally taste her, her gasp sends a surge of desire through me. The taste of her—the *smell* of her. I bury my face between her thighs and groan with every lap of my tongue through her folds.

Her hips lift from the bed as my attention—and tongue—aims for her throbbing clit. Wet and needy. When she starts to squirm, I lock my arms around her thighs and pin her between my mouth and the mattress. She whimpers and gasps, moving against my mouth. Grinding against my face.

"Beau," she moans, her hand darting out to fist my hair. The action spurs me on to unravel her completely.

I flatten my tongue over her clit, groaning as I flick and swirl over her sopping wet pussy. The tension in her body builds and she trembles. *She's close.* "Don't stop," she pleads. "Please, don't stop. Oh, Beau..."

I keep my pace, increasing the pressure ever so slightly that it causes her to break. She screams. Arching off the bed with a cry of my name as she comes beneath my tongue. *Fucking perfect.*

I stay with her through the aftershocks, gentling my touch as her breathing slowly steadies. When I finally move up her body, she pulls me down to her, kissing me deeply, tasting herself on my lips.

"Beau," she starts, her eyes twinkling. She laughs.

I brush her hair from her forehead, smiling down at her. "You're incredible."

"Me?" Her hands skim over my shoulders. "I think you're the incredible one."

"Glad you think so." I grin, slowly backing down her body for round two.

I wasn't lying when I said the taste of her was addictive.

Her playful smile turns to a gasp as I push her thighs upward, pinning them to her chest. Her pussy and ass lift to meet my watering mouth. I need to feel her come against my tongue again.

I fucking *crave* it.

Something permanent shifts inside me.

And I make her come and come and *come*...

Fifteen.

Callie

I WAKE UP ALONE and with a thrumming between my thighs that has me sighing.

Last night was... *Wow.*

Beau went down on me three—no, *four* times before he finally let me take a break. I thought we'd have sex after, or he'd at least want something from me, but I fell asleep naked in his arms.

The jerk *let me* fall asleep!

Now, as I lie here in bed still naked and spent, I try to piece together what happened. Or why more *didn't* happen?

Whiskey dick is my first assumption. Of course, that leads me to wonder how drunk he really was. Did he regret kissing me back? I mean, I did make the first move. Is he upset by that? Heck, does he remember any of it? Oh, god. What if he woke up and has no idea what happened?

I sit up in bed, startled as I hold a sheet to my chest, covering myself.

Did I...take advantage of him?

He was drunk. I was sober.

He told me to go back to sleep. I pulled him closer.

I kissed him...

He asked what we were doing.

I reach for my phone and rapidly text my fear process to Shea for clarification before realizing it's 9:07 AM. She's an hour behind me in California. No way is she awake this early on a Sunday. I drop my phone on the bed and run my hands through my tangled hair. That's when I notice Hulk isn't in his bed. The soft padding where he usually sleeps is empty.

Low voices drift through the door—Beau's deep rumble and another voice I don't recognize. I strain to hear what they're saying, but I can't make it out.

I slip out of bed, biting my lip at the remaining dampness between my legs, a reminder of just how *thorough* Beau was last night. I grab the first clothes I can find—my sleep shorts and Beau's T-shirt—and yank them on. I tiptoe to the bedroom door and crack it open just enough to peek through. Beau stands at the front door, his back to me as he signs something on a clipboard. Hulk is sitting awkwardly beside him, his leg cocked at an angle. He looks better this morning, more alert. The delivery person pushes a giant box—so large it barely fits through the door—at Beau, who nods his thanks.

I stare at him. Confused and concerned about what he's doing now. He's shirtless, wearing only yesterday's jeans that hang low on his hips. The muscles in his back flex as he maneuvers the enormous package inside, and I'm momentarily transfixed by the memory of those muscles moving above me, the way his skin felt under my fingertips.

The front door closes, and Beau turns toward the kitchen, pushing the box with him. That's when I notice it—or rather, the absence of it—the old stove that's been broken for weeks is *gone*.

Only a few dust bunnies remain as evidence that it was ever there.

I push the door open wider and step into the living room. "Beau?"

He turns, a slow grin lifting at the corner of his devilishly talented mouth. There's more stubble darkening his jaw than he usually has. It looks good on him. Too good.

"Morning."

I gesture to the massive package. "What is that?"

"This?" He pats the top of the box, his grin widening. "This is your new stove."

"My new—" I break off, stunned. "You bought me a *stove?*"

He laughs. "Yeah, well. Turns out, drunk me is surprisingly generous. I ordered it yesterday. Paid some ungodly amount for overnight shipping."

I walk closer, examining the box. Sure enough, it's a stainless-steel stove—the exact model I was eyeing online to match the fridge and microwave before my grumpy landlord told me *no*.

"But you said the replacement parts were coming," I say, running my hand along the box.

He shrugs, appearing sheepish all of a sudden. "I was being stubborn and cheap. The old one was beyond saving. And someone told me recently it was pretty fuckin' ugly."

Joy bubbles up inside me, and without thinking, I launch myself at him, throwing my arms around his neck and pressing my lips to his. For a brief, wonderful moment, his hands find my waist, but then he tenses beneath me.

I pull back, uncertainty flooding through me. *He doesn't remember.* I step back, putting a bit of space between us. "I'm sorry, I shouldn't have—"

His brows knit, gaze searching mine. "What's wrong?"

"Thank you for the stove. It's perfect, really. But I—I don't deserve it." I need to get this out in the open or it'll eat me alive. The words tumble out in a rush, "You were drunk and I kissed you and things went further than they should have and I-I took advantage of you when you weren't in a position to...you know...and I'm so, so sorry."

He stares at me for a long, silent moment, his expression unreadable. Then, to my complete surprise, he bursts out laughing. Not just a chuckle, either, but full-bodied laughter that has him bending over, hands on his knees, tears forming at the corners of his eyes.

"What's so funny?" I frown, feeling a bit defensive.

He tries to speak, but another wave of laughter takes him. Hulk looks between us, tail wagging uncertainly.

"Beau, if you don't stop laughing right this second..."

He finally straightens, wiping his eyes. "Sorry, sorry," he gasps, still fighting chuckles. "You think *you* took advantage of *me*?"

"Well, yes! You were drunk, and I was sober, and—"

He closes the distance between us, cupping my face in his hands. All humor is gone from his expression now, replaced by an intensity that makes my breath catch. "Callie," he says, his voice low and serious. "I wasn't that drunk. I knew exactly what I was doing last night. Every single moment of it."

"But you never—" I swallow hard. "You didn't let me touch you. You didn't want to—"

"Oh, trust me, I want to." His thumbs stroke over my cheekbones.

"Then why?" The question comes out as barely more than a whisper, my self-consciousness shining through.

His gaze softens. "It's been a while for me," he says. "And if it ever leads to that again, I don't want there to be any regrets."

I stare at him, speechless. This isn't the gruff, emotionally unavailable Beau I've come to know. This is someone else entirely. Someone vulnerable and honest and so much more than I ever expected.

"So, we're okay?" I ask, needing to be sure.

In answer, he leans down and kisses me, soft and sweet and full of promise. When he pulls back, there's a smile playing on his lips. "You can take advantage of me anytime, sweetheart."

I scoff, slapping him playfully on the arm. He laughs, pulling me against his chest. I can't help the smile that spreads across my face. "I'll remember that for next time," I quip, then glance at the massive box beside us. "I suppose if we want breakfast, we should install this thing."

His gaze darkens and he grips my ass as he kisses me. His lips are sure and firm against mine. He kneads my ass in his rough hands as his tongue delves into my mouth. Greedy and yearning. I melt into him.

I will never tire of this man's mouth.

When he pulls away, I'm gasping for air and begging for more. "What was that for?"

"The thought of you," he groans the words, "making me breakfast and wearing nothing but that dog-themed apron you have hanging behind you."

I glance over my shoulder at the apron in question and look back at him with a giggle, my hands running over his chest. "That could be arranged."

Beau growls low, his girth growing against my stomach. "I'll tell you what, help me get this set up, and afterward, I'll have *you* for breakfast instead."

Four times, Callie. Four *times.*

I bite my lip. "Deal."

His answering smile is wicked and...

A sudden knock at the door has me jumping into Beau's arms. I whip my head around, startled. Hulk barks, hobbling toward me. I shush him as I break away from Beau's embrace and head for the window. "Did you order anything else?" I ask over my shoulder.

"No," he grunts, following closely.

My stomach drops as I peer behind the curtain. What is he doing here? "Shit."

"Who is it?"

"My dad," I hiss, whipping around with wide eyes. If he sees me like this, I'll never hear the end of it. "You need to go."

Beau stiffens. "What?"

Panicked, I push him gently, urging him toward the back door. "Please."

He grabs my forearms, his expression crestfallen and hard. No longer the playful, sexy Beau from a moment ago. "No."

"Beau," I whine. "You don't understand. My father is—"

"Callie," Dad calls from the other side of the door. He knocks again. Harder this time. "Open the door. I know you're in there."

I stare at Beau with pleading eyes, but his stance remains firm. His jaw ticking in what I can only assume is anger. I don't blame him for being angry. I'm not prepared to explain this unexplainable thing that's barely begun between us.

I may be twenty-eight, but Matthew Ryan still sees me as a gullible, naïve teenager who saw the world through rose-colored glasses.

At the sound of another knock, I call back, "One second." I whip off Beau's shirt and toss it to him, then make a beeline for my bedroom, wincing as the rushed movement twinges my ankle without the walking boot on. I grab the nearest sweater I can find and pull it over my head before returning to the front door. Beau's chest is covered—*thank god*—and I spare him one last pleading look.

His stance is firm. The stubborn jerk even crosses his arms over his annoyingly yummy chest just to make it *one-thousand-percent* clear he's *not* leaving.

Fine. If he wants to meet him, he'll meet him all right.

I take a deep breath and open the door. My father stands tall and rigid on my front porch, his usual salt and pepper hair sporting more salt these days. Slacks and a tucked-in polo complete his overbearing father attire. His height is comparable to the asshat behind me. Although my father is slimmer, not as broad, or muscular.

But he has all the bite of a California rattlesnake to make up for it.

Dad's expression morphs three times in the span of a second. Annoyance to relief to suspicion. "Cal," he starts, his gaze shifting between my face and beyond.

"Hi, Dad." I pain a smile—and that's exactly what it feels like: *pain*. "I didn't know you were coming."

He harrumphs. "Are you going to invite me in?"

He doesn't respond to my query or acknowledge that I have company. He's here for a reason, and there's no stopping him when his mind is set.

"Right." I force a laugh, waving him in. "Silly me. I must still be waking up. Come in."

Dad steps inside, his sharp eyes immediately taking inventory of the cabin. They zero in on Beau standing near the kitchen with his arms still crossed, looking every bit the intimidating mountain man he can be when he wants to.

"Dad, this is Beau," I say, my voice artificially bright. "He's my...landlord." The word tastes sour in my mouth after what we shared last night and this morning.

Beau's stoic expression never falters. He extends a hand to my father, his voice clipped and formal—nothing like the warm, teasing tone he used with me. "Beau Montgomery."

Dad shakes his hand, sizing him up. "Matthew Ryan. Callie's father."

"Good to meet you, sir."

The silence stretches uncomfortably. Beau's jaw is tight, and I can practically *feel* the tension radiating off him. This isn't the flirtatious, affectionate man who was promising me another round of orgasms a few minutes ago.

"Beau is, um, here to install my new stove," I say quickly, gesturing toward the box. "The old one finally gave up."

Dad huffs, eyeing Beau. "I see. Well, that's convenient timing." He continues, turning to me, "We'll have breakfast in town while he works. Give him some space to get the job done."

I blink. "Oh, um, I— Sure. That sounds good." I glance at Beau out of the corner of my eye, hoping to gauge his reaction, but his expression remains unreadable. "I need to shower and get ready first," I add.

Beau clears his throat. "Actually, I have to run a few errands this morning. I'll be back shortly and have this put in before you get back."

My heart sinks. It's obviously a lie, but I can't exactly call him out on it in front of my father. "Of course," I manage, trying to keep the disappointment out of my voice.

Beau's face is neutral—professional, even—as he pulls on his boots by the door. I'm painfully aware of how he avoids looking at me. The easy intimacy we shared is gone, replaced by a wall I recognize all too well.

"It was nice meeting you, Mr. Ryan," Beau says, nodding to my father.

"Likewise."

Beau finally looks at me, and the coolness in his eyes makes my chest ache. He reaches for the door, and I follow, desperate to say something, anything, to fix whatever just fell off course between us.

"Beau," I start, but he's already outside and down the porch steps.

"Enjoy your breakfast," he says without looking back, his shoulders rigid.

I stand in the doorway, watching him hop in his truck and leave to put as much distance between us as possible.

He's my landlord. Stupid, stupid, stupid. Why couldn't I say he's a friend? A *good* friend? What I should've said is, *Dad, this is the man who saved Hulk and me.* Gushed about him, maybe. Said he's been taking care of me, sort of.

I did none of that.

Instead, I gave him the worst title anyone could be described as: Landlord.

"Callie?"

Dad's voice snaps me back to reality. I close the door and turn around, forcing another smile. "Sorry," I say, my voice steadier than how I feel. "I'll just be a minute." I need to shower, to think, to figure out how to approach Beau after this. Unfortunately, it'll have to wait. For now, I have to deal with my father, and whatever reason he has for this unannounced visit.

"Take your time," Dad says, settling onto the couch. Hulk follows, eager to greet the long-familiar human.

At least someone's happy about this visit.

I walk to the bedroom, my mind racing as the door closes behind me.

How did everything go from perfect to completely screwed up in minutes?

Sixteen.

Callie

"I'll take the lumberjack special," Dad tells the waitress, his hands folded on the red checkered tablecloth. "Pancakes, eggs over easy, bacon, sausage, hash browns. The works."

The waitress, a woman in her fifties with kind eyes and greying hair pulled back in a low ponytail, scribbles on her notepad. "And for you, honey?"

I glance at the menu one more time, though I haven't been reading it. My mind keeps drifting to the way Beau reacted when I called him my landlord, the deliberate distance he put between us afterward. "I'll have the same, please."

"Two lumberjacks coming right up." She collects our menus with practiced efficiency. "Coffee's fresh if you want a refill."

"Please," Dad says, sliding his mug toward the edge of the table.

She tops off our cups and heads toward the kitchen, leaving us alone in the corner booth of Murphy's Diner. The morning rush has died down, and only a few patrons occupy the scattered tables. Somewhere behind the counter, bacon sizzles on the grill, mingling with the scent of coffee and maple syrup.

I wrap my hands around my mug, using the warmth to steady myself. Dad studies me across the table, taking in details I wish he wouldn't. Like the fact I clearly wasn't expecting company this morning. And how Beau was there.

"Hulk seems to be handling his injury well," he says, dumping another cream into his coffee.

"The pain meds are helping."

Dad nods. "And you? I notice there isn't any swelling around your stitches and you're faring well enough with the walking boot."

Is that why he's here? "I appreciate your concern, but you didn't need to come all the way out here to check on me. I'm fine, Dad."

He takes a sip of his coffee, eyeing me over the rim. "I'm glad to see it for myself," he says. "Though I admit, I was also interested to finally see this town you ran off to."

There it is. The subtle dig about me 'running away' from California when things got too hard. I bite back my knee-jerk response and force myself to stay calm. "I didn't run off anywhere. I made a choice."

He doesn't argue, but his demeanor speaks volumes. "Well, regardless of why you're here, you seem healthy. Relaxed."

The waitress appears with our plates, setting down heaping portions of breakfast staples. The pancakes are the size of dinner plates, stacked three high, with eggs, bacon, and sausage crowding the rest of the space. Hash browns spill over onto a separate plate.

"Anything else I can get you folks?" she asks.

A doggy bag, for sure.

"We're set. Thank you," Dad says, reaching for the syrup.

We eat in relative silence for a while, the comfortable kind that comes from years of shared meals. Dad eats with methodical efficiency while I pick at mine.

When he's about halfway through, he sets his fork down. "So, about the premiere."

My stomach drops. "What about it?"

"Well, with Hulk being laid up and all, I've arranged for someone to escort you," he says casually, like we're discussing the weather.

"You've arranged..." I set down my fork and sigh. "Dad, I don't need an escort." I do, but it certainly won't be anyone my father chooses. Or god forbid, works with.

"You're not fooling anyone, Cal. You can't go alone. And I understand how important this premiere is to you. Not that I've ever understood the draw of horror films, what with the everyday horrors one can simply witness on the street." He takes another bite of pancakes as if he didn't just insult my career path. It wouldn't be the first time. "Deputy White is a good choice. Nice boy who can handle any security concerns."

Justin White. Of course, it's him. The overeager deputy who my father's become 'buddy-buddy' with that he's been sending out to 'check in' on me whenever he deems necessary. "You've got to be kidding me."

"He's responsible, respectful. He can protect you if needed." Dad's voice takes on that no-nonsense tone I remember from childhood. "And let's face it, Cal. Hulk isn't going to be around forever."

The casual way he says it hits me like a slap. I gape at him. "How can you say that?"

"It's the truth. Hulk's getting older—"

"He's *five*."

"—you can't rely on him for everything." He leans back in the booth, crossing his arms. "It's time you started thinking about finding someone who can be there for you long-term."

I stare at him, appalled. "Are you *seriously* trying to set me up right now?" Of all the people in my life—the very few of them—my father is the *last* person I would expect to pull something like this.

Shea? Oh, she's tried.

My *dad*? If pigs could fly!

"I'm trying to look out for you." His expression softens, but his words still sting. "Look, honey, I know this move to Montana wasn't what you wanted, but finding someone decent to settle down with could be the one good thing that comes out of it."

The one good thing. As if everything else about my life here doesn't matter. As if the only thing that could *possibly* make my 'running away' worthwhile would be landing a man.

"Dad. I didn't move here to find a husband. I moved here to get my life back."

He sighs, the sound heavy with frustration. "And you have. But you can't hide out forever, appearing only when it's convenient. You're twenty-eight years old. Most girls your age—"

"Most girls my age aren't paranoid, living in fear of being stalked." The words come out louder than I mean them to, and I glance around to make sure no one's listening. "Most girls my age haven't accomplished half the things I have, Dad."

He huffs. "You know what I mean."

"Do I? Because it sounds like you don't approve of how I'm living *my* life," I sneer. "How many times do we need to have this discussion before you'll leave it alone?"

His expression hardens. "You need someone stable who can protect you."

I fall back in my seat, my appetite gone. "And let me guess, your pet deputy is that someone."

"I've been told Justin is single and finds you very attractive."

I cringe at the salesman's pitch he's giving on this guy. "Jesus, Dad." I'm going to have nightmares after this, I know it. "That doesn't mean I want to date him."

"So, what, you're just going to be alone forever?"

The dismissive way he talks about my life choices makes my chest tight. Would he even be saying any of this if he knew I plan to ask Beau to come with me? "What if I am? What's wrong with being alone if that's what makes me feel safe?" I demand.

"Is that what you really want?" he counters, leaning forward. "Or are you just scared?"

The question hits too close to home, especially after this morning and the way I panicked when he showed up. How I couldn't bring myself to introduce Beau as anything more than my landlord.

He's so much more than that.

I sit up straight, my mind set. "This entire argument is pointless," I say, voice steady. "I already have someone attending the premiere and all the subsequent events and interviews with me. He won't be leaving my side. And—I'll have you know—he'll do a far better job at keeping me safe than Justin ever could."

His brow furrows, gaze searching mine. "Who?"

"Beau Montgomery."

Seventeen.

Beau

The nail gun *pops* three times as I press the trigger, securing another section of wall framing into place. The rhythm of the work keeps my mind off this morning and the way Callie's face went white when her father showed up. How quickly she reduced me to nothing more than a damn *landlord*.

Even if that is all I am to her. It shouldn't have fucking hurt the way it did to hear her say it.

I step back to check the frame's alignment, wiping sweat from my forehead with the back of my arm. The Montana sun beats down relentlessly. I pull my shirt over my head and toss it to the side. My boots crunch on wood shavings scattered across the foundation.

"Looking good, man."

I turn. Rhett's walking up the gravel path, his hands shoved in his jean pockets. I grunt, not in the mood for any brotherly banter. After the last week, I've had my fill for the rest of the fucking year. I shift my attention back to the frame and heft another two-by-four into position.

He stops a few feet away. "This place is coming along."

I line up the board and reach for the nail gun. *Pop, pop, pop.*

"Everything okay?" he asks.

"I'm working."

He's quiet for a moment, likely waiting for me to entertain him or stop to chat. He'll be here a while if that's what he's after. "Right. Well, I just stopped by to grab a few things from last night."

"Door's open," I tell him.

He kicks at a wood scrap with the toe of his boot, continuing to linger and watch my every move. "You sure you're good? You seem a little..."

"Fine," I bite out, glaring at him over my shoulder as I reload the nail gun with another set.

"This wouldn't have anything to do with the blonde next door, would it?"

My hand tightens on the nail gun. "Don't know what you're talking about."

"Duke told me about what happened. I guess Maci told him how you saved Callie on the trail," he says cooly. When I ignore his obvious grab for my attention, he continues, "So the fact you're out here building like your life depends on it at noon on a Sunday has nothing to do with her or...?"

I set down the nail gun and reach for my water bottle, taking a long swig to buy myself time. "Her father showed up this morning," I say. I don't know why the hell I tell him that. It's none of his or anyone else's business, but the words come out regardless.

"And?"

"She introduced me as her landlord." The title spits between my lips and I realize the moment had a greater effect on me than I care to acknowledge. But what can I say? She was freaking out, begging me to leave out the back, and I refused. It's my own damn fault. I asked for it.

Rhett's quiet for a moment. "That sting a little?"

More than a little, but like everything, I brush it off. "It's the truth."

My brother looks at me with pity. "Man, I get—"

The crunch of tires on gravel cuts him off. A dark sedan pulls in. Through the windshield, I can make out two figures—Callie and her father.

The car idles for a moment before the passenger door opens and Callie steps out with a to-go bag in hand. She says something to her father through the open window, then steps back and waves as he pulls away. For a moment, she just stands there watching the car disappear down the road.

Then she turns and looks directly at me.

Even from this distance, I can see the hesitation in her posture before she starts walking toward me. Her gait is still slightly uneven from the walking boot.

"Shit," I mutter under my breath.

Rhett crosses his arms like he's settling in to watch the show.

She reaches the edge of the construction site and stops, her gaze shifting between Rhett and me. "Hi," she says, uncertain. "Beau, can we talk?"

My shoulders lock up tight, every muscle in my back going rigid as I force myself to keep working. "Stove is in," I grunt, deliberately turning my back to her as I set my water down to move the final pieces of frame where I'll need them. "Works good. Might still be cooling down, so be careful."

"Oh, um, awesome." She smiles with tight lips, glancing at Rhett. "But that's not what I need to talk about."

"Nothing else to discuss," I mutter, avoiding eye contact.

"Dammit, Beau," she snaps, and I lift my gaze to find her glaring at me. When I do, her heated gaze softens. "I'm sorry, okay? I didn't mean to hurt you."

You did. The words hit like a punch to the gut. "You didn't."

She sighs. "Well, I'm sorry anyway. My dad can be...overbearing. And after last night, we didn't have a chance to talk and... I'd really like to talk."

"What happened last night?" Rhett chimes in as nonchalant and nosey as ever.

This fuckin' family, I swear.

I scowl in his direction. "Don't you have somewhere else to be?"

He grins. "Nope."

I huff my frustration.

"Listen, I don't know how to broach this subject with you, so I'll just come right out and say it," she says, grabbing my attention as she takes a deep breath.

My pulse jumps.

"I need you to come to California with me for two weeks, and you have to say yes because I already told my dad you're coming, and I *really* don't want to have to go with Justin. I'll pay for everything. All you have to do is never leave my side. No orgasms required."

Rhett coughs, seeming to choke on nothing but air.

Something claws at my chest, demanding I go to her. I fight to shut it down and stand firm.

"I leave for the premiere in less than three weeks," she says, her lower lip wobbling. "Hulk might be walking fine by then, but he won't be well enough to fly or handle the long days. I need backup. I need...you."

"Callie." I don't know what she wants me to say here. To tell her that every word out of her mouth is making it harder to stay away—to protect myself.

"I'll pay you," she offers. "You'd be acting as my personal bodyguard and lead any security details attending my events. Name your price."

You. You're my price. I want you, lodges in my throat. I swallow them down. "I don't want your money."

Tears are welling in her eyes now. "Please, Beau."

I run a hand over my face. The urge to say yes is overwhelming. Two weeks beside her, away from prying eyes and open ears. Just her and me. It could be exactly what I need to figure out what this is between us.

Or she'll hate me by the end of it all.

"I'll think about it."

She sniffles, nodding quickly.

I watch her turn away and walk to her cabin. I take a half-step toward her before I force myself to stay put. The war between what I want and what I think I should do tears at my gut as her door closes behind her.

The moment it does, Rhett throws a hammer at my head.

I duck. "The fuck, Rhett!"

"What the fuck is wrong with you?" he growls. His usual cool demeanor—gone. Replaced by a kind of frustration I've never seen from him before. "You've been working yourself to the goddamn bone since you got back—not once taking a break to take care of yourself. You're fucking miserable. *Go.* Levi and I will work on the build while you're away if that's what you're worried about."

I sneer at him. "Mind your fucking—"

"*You* are my fucking business," he barks. "You think I keep showing up here for shits and giggles? No. You're my brother and I love you, but *fuck*, man. Everyone is worried about you and you couldn't care less. I've got Duke, Butch, Ma, Pop calling me every damn day asking how *you* are. You want to push everyone away? Fine. You want to tell me to go fuck myself? Wouldn't be the first time." His face reddens in anger. "But don't you fucking dare turn that woman away because you're too goddamn proud to feel something for someone."

My jaw tightens as the truth of his words rains over me. He's right, and I hate him for it. The armor I've built around myself to keep from getting too close to anyone isn't protection any longer—it's destruction. I'm pushing away the one person who makes me want to tear it all down.

Rhett shakes his head at me, and without another word, walks to his truck and leaves.

I know what I have to do. I've been so busy protecting my heart that I've forgotten what it feels like to actually use it.

It's time I changed that.

Eighteen.

Callie

HULK'S HEAD TRAILS ME as I pace the short span of my living room, biting my nails and fighting back tears. Beau and Rhett are arguing outside, but I can't make out what they're saying.

God, I handled that so badly. Ambushing him like that, in front of his brother, with my desperate plea and my stupid joke about orgasms. I cringe at the memory as I pace, wearing a path in the hardwood floor.

The voices outside grow louder for a moment, then suddenly cut off. A truck door slams, followed by an engine starting. I freeze mid-step, straining to listen as the vehicle pulls away. I wait for something to tell me what just happened, but there's only silence.

Did Beau leave, too? Or is he going back to work, writing me off as the desperate, broken tenant who can't handle her own life? I sink onto the couch and angrily tear off my useless walking boot that's pinching my calf yet again. It hits the ground with a thud, and I bury my face in my hands. Hulk whines softly and limps over, resting his massive head on my knee. "I really screwed this up, didn't I, buddy?" I whisper, scratching behind his ears.

The front door crashes open without warning.

Hulk barks, and I jump, my heart in my throat. My head whips to face the door where Beau's broad stance fills the entryway. His bare chest rises and falls rapidly. There's something wild in his dark eyes—raw and determined. A man possessed.

I stand as he steps inside, shutting the door behind him. His gaze never leaves mine as he says roughly, "Yes."

I blink. "What?"

He walks closer, each step deliberate. "I'll go with you. To California. All of it."

Relief hits me so hard my knees nearly buckle. "Beau—"

"But we're done pretending there isn't something here between us." He stops just inches away, close enough that I can see the need in his eyes. The way his arms flex to reach for me.

I nod vigorously. "I'm so sorry, I didn't mean—"

"Not because of your father." He cups my face and his thumb brushes away a stray tear slipping down my cheek. "Because for a split second, I thought I was going to lose you before I ever truly had you."

His mouth crashes against mine. The kiss is greedy, hungry, full of all the attraction we've been dancing around for weeks. I melt into him. I grasp his shoulders, his skin hot to the touch as he backs me against the wall beside the bedroom door.

"I fucking want you, baby," he breathes against my lips. "More than anything. I want to be with you in every fucking way, and it's tearing me up inside how bad I need *you*."

My body ignites at his words, his rough tone, and the way he presses his hips into mine. "Yes," I whisper between kisses.

His hands slide down to grip my thighs, and suddenly I'm airborne. My legs wrap around his waist instinctively as he carries me through the bedroom doorway, his mouth never leaving mine. The kiss is desperate, consuming, like he's trying to pour everything he couldn't say into this moment.

He tosses me onto the bed with a primal growl that sends heat pooling between my thighs. I bounce once on the mattress, breathless and wanting, as he stands at the foot of the bed, his eyes devouring me.

"You're so fucking beautiful," he mutters, his fingers finding the hem of my shirt.

I lift my arms, helping him strip it off. The cool air kisses my skin, but I'm burning everywhere his molten gaze touches. His eyes darken at the sight of my lace bra, and I watch his throat work as he swallows when I remove it. My nipples harden under his stare.

His touch is surprisingly gentle as he slides up my sides, a stark contrast to the intensity in his expression. He unbuttons my jean shorts with deliberate slowness, dragging the zipper down tooth by tooth until I'm squirming beneath him. "Please," I pant.

"Patience," he murmurs, a smirk playing on his lips.

He peels my shorts down my legs, leaving me in just my underwear. I expect him to rush, to tear the remaining fabric from my body, but instead, he kneels at the edge of the bed and presses a kiss to my ankle, then another to my calf, moving upward with agonizing slowness.

"I've craved your taste all damn day, sweetheart," he confesses against my inner thigh, his breath hot against my skin.

I fist the duvet when his lips travel higher. The bristle along his jaw adds to the raw need building inside of me. His strong hands push my thighs apart and the look he gives me makes me feel worshipped rather than exposed.

"Beau," I whisper, a plea.

"I've got you," he promises. "Always."

He hooks one finger into the side of my panties, and his mouth is on me. I cry out at the first touch of his tongue, my back arching off the bed. He holds my hips firmly, keeping me in place as he devours me. Each stroke of his tongue sends electricity coursing through my veins. I'm trembling beneath his mouth. His touch.

When he slides a finger inside me, I nearly come off the bed.

"Fuck, you're so wet," he groans against me, the vibration of his words intensifying the sensation pulsing through my clit.

He tries to add a second finger, but I tense from the pinch of it.

"And fucking tight," he grunts.

He drops the second finger and curls the single digit inside me, rubbing. I see stars. The dual sensation of the pressure inside and his tongue flicking against my most sensitive spot is overwhelming.

My thighs begin to shake as tension coils tighter and tighter in my core.

"Mhmm," he encourages, his voice rough with desire as he sucks my clit.

I tip over the edge. Shatter with his name on my lips. My body convulses in waves of uncontrollable pleasure. And he doesn't stop—his fingers continue their relentless rhythm, his tongue circling and flicking until I'm climbing again, faster this time.

I gasp, overwhelmed by the sopping wet sound echoing between us.

"One more," he insists, looking at me with dark, determined eyes. "Give me one more and I'll let you wrap this perfect pussy around my cock, baby."

The second orgasm hits me even harder than the first, stealing my breath. I'm vaguely aware of crying out, of my body arching impossibly high off the bed, of my fingers gripping his hair. *Beau...*

As I float back to earth, trembling and gasping, he crawls up my body, pressing kisses to my stomach, between my breasts, along my collarbone. He's still clothed, the rough fabric of his jeans creating a delicious friction against my over-sensitized skin.

"I didn't know you had such a dirty mouth," I pant, tugging at his shirt.

"A lot you don't know about me," he says in a way that tears at my heart. His gaze locks with mine, and for a moment, I see that vulnerability again—that fear of letting someone in completely. He tries to mask it, but he can't. Not with me.

I pull him down and press my lips to his. "Let me see all of you, Beau."

When we part, he stares down at me. "No one's ever seen me," he admits roughly. "Not like you do."

I smile, bringing my hands up to slide around his neck. The corner of his mouth lifts and he kisses me. A slow, heartfelt promise made between us without a single word spoken.

He breaks the kiss and I drink in the sight of him—broad shoulders, muscled chest dusted with dark hair, and the tapestry of scars that tell the story of his life. I reach out to trace one that runs along his ribs, and he catches my hand, pressing it flat against his thundering heart.

He unbuckles his belt and pushes his jeans low on his thighs. His thick, vein-wrapped cock stands at attention. The head is smeared with glossy precum that pools at the tip as I gaze in appreciation. He's magnificent. All hard, bulky planes and strength, yet the way he watches me—unsure, hesitant—makes my heart twist.

"How long has it been?" I whisper, reaching for him.

He grunts as I wrap my hand around his length. He's hot and impossibly hard. "Four years," he hisses as I stroke him from base to tip.

I smile faintly, meeting his gaze. "Me, too."

He covers my body with his a second later. His weight presses me into the mattress in the most delicious way. He braces himself on his forearms, his face hovering above mine as he reaches down to toy with the damp seam of my pussy. I suck in a breath. "I don't have any protection," he growls, pushing my soaked panties to the side so he can circle my clit.

I arch into him with a moan. "I have the implant."

He grunts, "Good girl."

The head of his cock presses at my entrance, and I melt—at the endearment or the feel of his swollen head sliding through my folds, it's anyone's guess. *Both, definitely both.* His hips flex forward, testing. I wrap my legs around his waist in response, bringing him closer and forcing his cock to push inside me.

We moan together at the feeling of finally being joined.

Me, at being filled and stretched.

Him, doing the filling and stretching.

Without warning, my walls tighten around him and he curses under his breath. I cling to him as he sinks deeper and deeper. "Beau, *oh*—" I moan, gasping for air as his cock drags against my walls and the part of me only he can find.

"Fuck, sweetheart," he growls, jerking his hips and earning a squeak from me. "You're gonna come already, aren't you?" He picks up a slow, grinding rhythm and my legs fall farther open. The room fills with our shared sounds—his low groans mixing with my desperate moans. His eyes never leave mine, each thrust impossibly deep.

"Yes," I gasp, my fingernails digging into his shoulders as he picks up the pace. "Yes, yes, yes—"

His expression is intense as he watches me come undone beneath him. "That's it," he coaxes, his voice strained. "Come on my fuckin' cock."

The dirty demand from his usually guarded mouth sends electricity down my spine. I'm already so sensitive from his earlier attention that it takes embarrassingly little time before I'm teetering on the edge a third time.

"I can't—it's too much—" My words dissolve into incoherent sounds as another orgasm crashes through me. My inner walls clench around him in rhythmic pulses.

"Look at me," he commands, and I force myself to meet his gaze. The intimacy of his request—more than the physical sensation—is what undoes me. My fourth orgasm hits without warning, more powerful than any before. I cry out his name, my vision blurring at the edges as wave after wave of ecstasy washes over me.

"Fuck," he hisses, his pace faltering momentarily as my body grips him. "You're perfect. So fucking perfect." He buries his face in my neck, his breathing ragged against my skin, his restraint slipping—the carefully controlled man giving way to something more primal.

I want that. I want him to lose himself completely. For me.

"More," I demand, raking my nails down his back. "Harder."

With a growl that vibrates through my chest, he hooks one of my legs over his shoulder, changing the angle and driving deeper.

Words fail me as he fucks me with an intensity I can't describe. I cling to him as he pounds into me. The headboard slams against the wall with each thrust.

He drives into me one final time. He groans my name against my lips, his entire body tensing as he finds his release and empties inside me. Heat floods my core.

Careful not to crush me with his weight, he slips an arm beneath me and collapses beside me on the bed, bringing me with him. His cock still buried inside me.

I giggle and he grins.

We lie there panting, our skin slick with sweat, neither of us capable of speaking. My leg is thrown over his hip and his arm is draped heavily across my waist, his firm hand at the top of my ass. Minutes pass in comfortable silence. He traces gentle patterns on my lower back. The kind of tenderness I had no idea he had in him.

I love it.

"This isn't just sex for me," he says finally, his voice quiet but certain. "I need you to know that."

My heart swells at his honesty. "I know," I whisper. "It isn't for me, either."

He kisses me softly. "I'm still figuring out how to do this whole...relationship shit," he admits, then tenses. "That is, if that's what this is... Is it?"

I smile at him and have to laugh at the uncertainty in his eyes. "I sure hope so," I say, then ask, "How long has it been since you've been in a relationship?"

He huffs and shifts his gaze away from mine as he confesses, "High school."

"Ouch," I tease, then snuggle into him. "I'll give you a grace period. How's that sound?"

He presses a kiss to my forehead. "I'd appreciate that."

As we lie there, tangled in each other, I realize that whatever walls Beau had built around himself have not just cracked—they've come crashing down.

And in their place is something new and entirely *mine*.

Nineteen.

Beau

CALLIE AND I FALL into a pattern over the next three weeks. She spends her days with Hulk working on finishing some 'big project' she needs to have ready for some producer in LA, while I've been fighting to get this cabin build as close to done as I can before we go. We meet at the end of the day, share dinner, have sex, and I sleep better than I have in my entire life with her in my arms every night.

We're essentially living together, but neither of us broaches the subject officially—my duffle bag still packed and sitting on her bedroom floor. She even paid her rent on the first of the month last week. When I brought it up, she brushed me off with a *'fair is fair.'* Whatever the hell that means. I wanted to press her on it, but I dropped it instead.

I'm no relationship expert, but I think we may have skipped a step or two.

Not that I'm complaining.

It's 0700 and I've just pulled in to Duke's to drop off Hulk for the next two weeks. The early morning sun casts long shadows across the mountains, painting everything in a stunning golden Montana light.

I glance in the rearview mirror at Callie sitting in the backseat with him, her arm around Hulk and kissing the side of his massive head. Her eyes are red from crying. She cried all night and into the morning. Practically sleeping on his dog bed with him, we opted to bring him as close to the bed as possible.

Thankfully, Maci offered to dog sit. Duke was thrilled to use the moment as a test for life with a baby and a dog—something he's been begging Maci for. Rumor has it, Maci already bought him one for their anniversary; he just doesn't know it yet.

I park the truck and hop out, walking around to the back to grab Hulk's bed, food, dishes, and sack of toys.

"Morning," Duke calls, jogging toward me. With a huge grin on his face, he takes the grocery bags full of Hulk's premium dog food, frozen chicken, and painkillers. He hasn't needed them as much the last few weeks, and he's been walking like a champ, but Callie insisted we bring them just in case.

Her walking boot has been off for weeks as well, and with a bit of makeup, the thin red line by her temple is invisible. You'd never know she took a hell of a fall less than a month ago as she hops out in a form-fitting summer dress that's had me adjusting myself one too many times in the last hour.

"Morning," I say, nodding to the bed and bag in my hand. "Where do you want this?"

"Inside," my brother says with the giddy excitement of a school boy. I smirk. "I cleared him a spot in the living room. I even got him a bed for my office at work."

"That's really sweet of you." Callie sniffles as she helps Hulk down from the backseat. The hair on his hind leg is growing in faster than I thought it would. "Thank you again for doing this."

Duke grins. "Are you kidding me? I should be thanking you for thinking of us," he tells her. "Olivia is going to be thrilled. Maci even commented that she's interested to see how a big dog will fit in with our routine and the house."

"Sounds like you might be getting your wish soon," I comment. Callie nudges me with her elbow and glares.

My brother shrugs. "A man can dream."

We follow Duke inside his two-story, custom-built mountainside home and enter through the kitchen, where Olivia is perched in her highchair having breakfast.

Maci stands at the sink, smiling at our arrival. "Good morning," she calls.

Olivia squeals the moment she lays eyes on Hulk, her arms flailing with excitement. His tail wags vigorously as he trails beside Callie to say hello. The baby giggles that flood the room put a smile on everyone's face.

I wait off to the side as Callie talks through Hulk's schedule and his trained cues for needing to go out or if he may be in pain. She hands them a written report she's been working on all week, reiterating everything she just told them. "If anything comes up, *please* call me," she says finally. "You have my number and Beau's, but I also wrote down my friend Shea's, my father's, and my assistant's."

Maci's brow furrows as she looks over the three sheets of paper in hand. "You have an assistant?"

"Production assistant," she says. "She'll have my phone and such during interviews and the premiere."

Duke snorts, impressed. "Sounds fancy."

Callie laughs. "Well, it is LA."

I clear my throat, noting the time. "We need to head out if we're going to make the flight."

Hulk is sitting next to Olivia's highchair, content as can be as Callie crouches beside him. She kisses him and he licks her tear-streaked face.

"You be a good boy, okay?" Her lower lip wobbles. "I'll be back in two weeks. And we'll video chat every night. I love you so much, big boy." She hugs him one last time before standing with a choked cry.

She turns with a sniffle, meets my gaze, and walks right into my arms. I hold her as she buries her face in my chest, clinging to me...in front of my brother and sister-in-law.

Something tightens in my chest—a mixture of protectiveness and something else I'm still getting used to when it comes to Callie. Six weeks ago, I would've stiffened at this public display. Now, I find myself stroking her hair, not giving a damn who sees it. Though I try to ignore the raised brow of my brother and the beaming smile from his wife.

We haven't exactly been open about what's been going on between us over the last few weeks. Another step in this relationship I feel like we missed. Or maybe I'm reading too far into it? None of my family has seen us together. Not even Rhett, who's stopped asking altogether when he does come around to check in.

We give our goodbyes and I lead Callie to the truck, helping her into the front seat. I soak in the crisp morning air. In a few hours, we'll be in her world instead of mine. *A world she fears.*

The thought sends an unexpected ripple of tension through my shoulders.

"Hey, Beau," Duke shouts, jogging toward me.

I close Callie's door and turn to him. "Yeah?"

He pants with a grin. "I wanted to, uh, make sure you knew you have a plus one for the wedding next month."

Right. The double wedding. The thought of Callie at my side during an important family event hits differently than I expected. It feels right. I lock the topic away for later.

"Good to know," I say, starting to walk around to the driver's side. I hop in and back out, glaring at my brother and his shit eatin' grin as he waves before backpedaling to the house.

The ride to the airport on the other side of town is silent aside from Callie's occasional sniffle.

"How you holding up over there?" I ask, glancing between her and the road. In the distance, I can see the airport—a tiny building compared to what we'll land at in Los Angeles. I've been to some big cities during my service, but never to play bodyguard for someone I'm falling for.

Falling for? Ah, fuck.

"I'm okay," she says quietly. "And before you say it, I know he's in good hands."

I bark a laugh. "As long as you already know."

She smiles—the first one I've seen from her in days. It eases something in me I didn't realize was wound tight.

I pull into the long-term airport parking lot, a gravel patch with painted lines. The terminal is a single-story building in the middle of a wide stretch of pavement. A few small commuter planes sit on the tarmac, and I mentally prep myself for the cramped seats and knee pain when Callie points to the far end of the runway.

"We need to go there," she says, gesturing toward a sleek white jet sitting by itself.

I slow the truck to a stop. "Where?"

"That's our plane." Her voice is casual, like she's commenting on the weather.

I squint at the private jet gleaming in the morning sun. "That's...not a commercial flight," I say, confused.

"No," she agrees, a hint of amusement creeping into her voice. Her eyes are still red-rimmed but now containing a spark of mischief. "Did I forget to mention that part?"

"You might have left out a detail or two," I mutter, putting the truck back in drive and following her directions toward the separate entrance and parking area.

As we pull up, a man in a crisp uniform approaches. I park where he indicates and step out, on alert. This is the first time Callie and I have been out together, just the two of us. I need to make sure she knows she can count on me the same way she counts on Hulk on any given day. And that starts *now*.

Callie slides out, and the man's professional demeanor breaks into a wide smile. "Miss Ryan," he greets her warmly. "It's wonderful to see you again."

"You, too, Marcus," she replies, accepting his brief hug. "This is Beau," she adds, gesturing to me. "He's with me. Hulk is on leave for this trip."

Marcus extends his hand. "Pleasure to meet you, sir. I'll take care of your bags."

I shake his hand, then help him unload our luggage from the truck bed. Callie takes her carry-on and waits for me, shifting her weight from one foot to the other.

"You fly private a lot?" I ask as we follow Marcus toward the jet.

She shrugs. "The studio arranges it for premieres and press tours. Less hassle, no paparazzi at commercial terminals. And they respect that I usually have Hulk with me."

"Right."

The amusement in her eyes grows. "You look a little shell-shocked."

I scoff. "Just trying to figure out how different the next few weeks are going to be."

That earns me a genuine laugh. She loops her arm through mine. "Don't worry. I don't expect you to keep up with Hollywood appearances or expenses. But fair warning, my designer has several outfits and suits for you to try when we arrive."

"Noted," I say, mentally recalibrating what the next two weeks might look like.

We approach the aircraft where a small set of stairs has been extended to the ground. At the top stands a woman in a navy uniform, her blonde hair pulled back in a neat bun. "Good morning, Miss Ryan," she says with a professional smile. "Welcome aboard."

"Thanks, Brittany," Callie replies. "This is Beau. He's a bit new to all this."

Brittany nods to me. "First time on a private jet, Mr...?"

"Montgomery," I say. "And yeah, usually I'm wedged between two guys about my size in military transport."

"Well, I think you'll find this much more comfortable," Brittany says with a wink. "Please, come aboard."

I let Callie go first, my hand finding the small of her back as she climbs the stairs. The interior of the jet is nothing like I expected—all cream leather seats and polished wood. It's more like a living room than an aircraft.

"Drinks after takeoff?" Brittany asks.

"Coffee would be great," Callie responds, settling into one of the plush seats. She looks at me still standing and taking it all in. "Beau?"

"Coffee," I echo, finally lowering myself into the seat beside her. "Black."

As Brittany moves toward the galley, I lean in close to Callie. "Anything else you forgot to mention?"

She bites her lip. "I may have downplayed things a bit."

"A bit," I repeat, raising a brow at the luxury surrounding us.

The pilot emerges from the cockpit. "Miss Ryan, good to see you. We're cleared for takeoff in about ten minutes."

"Thanks, Tim," she says. "This is Beau."

We exchange nods, and Tim returns to the cockpit. Brittany secures the door, and the engines begin to hum.

"No safety demonstration?" I ask.

Callie shakes her head. "Not necessary. Basically, don't unbuckle when the light is on, and if we crash, those are the emergency exits," she points toward two doors.

"Comforting," I mutter.

She takes my hand, her earlier sadness momentarily replaced by gentle teasing. "Don't tell me the big, bad ex-military man is afraid of flying?"

"Not afraid," I correct her. "Just prefer having a parachute when I'm this high up."

She squeezes my hand. "You've jumped out of planes?"

"That's classified," I say with a straight face, then crack a smile when her eyes widen. "Yes, many times."

The jet begins to taxi, and her grip tightens slightly. For all her casual familiarity with this world, there's a subtle tension in her shoulders as we accelerate down the runway. "Nervous?"

She gives me a half-smile. "Not about flying. Just...everything else."

I slide my hand over her thigh and squeeze. "That's what I'm here for."

She slides her arm around mine and leans her head against my shoulder as the jet lifts smoothly into the air. "Is that all you are?"

The question hangs between us, loaded with everything we haven't formally defined. "No," I say simply, pressing a kiss to the top of her head. "That's not all I am, sweetheart."

Twenty.

Callie

"Shea is picking us up. We'll probably grab lunch before she takes us to the hotel," I tell Beau when the plane touches down in California. It's a little after eleven and I'm starving. "She's my best friend, so be nice."

He gives me a scowly look. "I am nice."

I snort a laugh and pat his hand still on my thigh. It hasn't moved an inch the entire flight. "When meeting new people? Sure, you are, sweetie."

He huffs.

"I also texted you our itinerary for tomorrow," I say. "Today is more of a down day. Get settled in, outfit prep, relax before the crazy."

"How crazy are we talking?" he asks, unbuckling his seatbelt as the plane taxies to a stop.

"Scale of one to ten?" I consider. "Tomorrow's probably a six. Premiere night will be a solid ten for me."

He nods once, processing. "And what exactly happens at a premiere?"

"Red carpet, photographers, interviews, watching the film, after-party." I count off on my fingers. "Standard Hollywood stuff."

"Right."

I press a kiss to his jaw, loving the slight stubble against my lips. "You'll be perfect. The camera is going to love you," I say, trying to lighten the mood.

Beau tends to be hard to read at times, and I'm battling to decipher if he's nervous or simply taking this trip very, *very* seriously.

"I'm not here to be loved," he reminds me, but his expression softens. "I'm here for you."

Same thing, I want to say, but bite my tongue.

Brittany appears to inform us that we can disembark. Beau stands, stretching his long frame in the confined space, his movement favoring his left, a subtle reminder of his knee injury. I make a mental note to ask him about it later.

He offers me his hand—a small gesture that anchors me as we step off the plane into the California sunshine. The private terminal at LAX is designed for discretion, but I still scan the area out of habit, looking for unwanted cameras or faces. Instead, I spot Shea waving enthusiastically from beside a sleek black SUV.

"There she is," I say, squeezing Beau's hand.

Shea bounces toward us, designer sunglasses perched on top of her head, pushing back her voluminous curls. She's wearing what passes for casual in LA—crisp white linen pants and a silky blue top.

"Cals!" she squeals, throwing her arms around me. "Finally! I thought Montana might have permanently claimed you."

Dramatic as always.

I hug her back tightly, realizing how much I've missed her. "Not yet," I laugh.

She pulls back, holding me at arm's length. "You look...different." Her perfectly shaped brows lift as she takes me in. Her gaze shifts to Beau standing behind me. "And this must be the reason why."

I turn to Beau, whose expression has settled into what I've come to think of as his *public face*: guarded and far too serious. "Shea, this is Beau Montgomery. Beau, this is my best friend, Shea Winton."

Beau takes her hand. "Nice to meet you."

Shea's eyes widen slightly at the sound of his deep voice, and I recognize the approving once-over she gives him. "You, too. Welcome to LA. I hope you're ready for the Hollywood experience." She links her arm through mine, leading us toward the SUV. "I made us reservations at Ivy by the Shore. I figured you'd want something with outdoor seating after being cooped up in Montana."

"I wasn't cooped up," I protest with a roll of my eyes. "Montana has more open space than all of California."

"Yes, but does it have proper sushi?" Shea counters.

I glance back at Beau—his gaze trained on me.

The driver takes our bags and loads them into the trunk while we slide into the backseat, Shea sitting across from us in the custom SUV. "So, Beau," she says once we're settled. "Callie tells me the third cabin project is coming along. Still on track to finish before winter?"

Beau nods. "Structure is done. Interior work is what takes time."

"I'd love to see pictures," Shea says with genuine interest. "I've been thinking about branching out more into interior design. Fashion's been..." she waves her hand vaguely, "feeling a bit stale lately."

"Really?" I ask, surprised. In all of our phone conversations and text chains, she hasn't once mentioned interior design as anything more than a hobby or consulting for her father's hotels. "You're one of the most successful designers in LA, though."

She sighs. "That's the problem. I've been playing it safe. Staying in my lane. What I really want to do is flip a house—something with character that I can completely transform. Blend fashion sensibility with architectural elements."

I smile at the enthusiasm in her tone. "You do love a good *House Flipper* episode."

Shea laughs. "I do."

"You should talk to Rhett," Beau suggests unexpectedly. "My brother. He's been big on renovations lately. Fixing up a lot of the older homes in Whitetail. He owns a construction company with our younger brother, Levi."

Shea's eyes light up. "I'd love that. Maybe I should visit this small town of yours."

"You'd hate it," I tease. "The closest mall is an hour away."

"I can rough it," she insists with a smile that suggests otherwise. "For research purposes."

As the car navigates through LA traffic, Shea updates me on industry gossip and fills Beau in on what to expect over the next few weeks—where to stand, who to watch out for, which reporters to avoid.

"The good news is, most of them will respect the security angle," she tells him. "They're used to celebrities bringing personal protection. Just look stern and professional, and they'll leave you alone."

"That's his default setting," I say, earning a side-eye from Beau.

I watch him take in the unfamiliar landscape of palm trees and sprawling mansions. This is my world, not his, and I'm dying to hear his thoughts.

The car pulls up to the restaurant, a breezy beachside place with white trellises covered in climbing flowers. When we exit the vehicle, Beau scans the surroundings, his gaze tracking the people nearby.

"This place is known for being paparazzi-free. That's why Shea picked it," I tell him quietly as a thought comes to me. "Have you had sushi before?"

He looks down at me and smirks. "For you, I'll try it."

I bite my lip to keep from smiling too big. His hand settles protectively at the small of my back as we follow the host to our table on the terrace overlooking the Pacific Ocean.

"So," Shea says as we take our seats, "tell me more about this cabin. What's your vision for the interior?" She directs this at Beau, and I can tell it's a deliberate choice to engage with him—and I love her for it.

As Beau begins describing the open-concept living space and stone fireplace he's planning, I watch Shea's genuine interest in his answers, the way she asks follow-up questions about materials and light exposure. They continue talking and I feel a strange collision of my worlds—the Hollywood life I've been avoiding and the Montana sanctuary I've created.

Somehow, watching my best friend and Beau connect over renovation challenges, those worlds don't seem quite so separate anymore.

For the first time in months, I'm not sure which one feels more like home. Or maybe it isn't about the place at all...

Because the man beside me somehow bridges both.

Twenty-One.

Beau

AFTER THE DRIVER DROPS Callie's friend off at her condo, he takes us to what has to be the fanciest hotel I've ever seen. Palm trees line the entire place and a red carpet leads to massive glass doors held open by men in crisp uniforms. Callie doesn't bat an eye when one takes our luggage and we're ushered through a grand lobby with marble floors and crystal chandeliers.

"Miss Ryan, welcome back," the concierge greets as we approach the front desk. "We've prepared the Presidential Suite as requested."

Presidential Suite? How successful *is* this movie?

I shift my weight, my knee beginning to throb after the flight and drive. I've been trying not to favor it, but Callie notices. She slips her hand into mine, a gentle squeeze that asks if I'm okay without words. I return the pressure, letting her know I'm fine.

"Your luggage has already been taken up," the concierge continues, passing Callie a key card. "And the packages from Miss Shea Winton arrived this morning."

"Thank you," she says with a warm smile—the kind that makes men trip over themselves to help her.

Her porch swing and brand-new stove come to mind.

We're escorted to a private elevator that whisks us to the top floor. The doors open directly into the suite, and I freeze in the entryway. The place is bigger than two of my larger cabins put together. Floor-to-ceiling windows showcase a panoramic view of Los Angeles, the ocean a distant blue line on the horizon. Everything is white marble, glass, and gold fixtures.

I search for the right word to describe the culture shock and end up with, "Christ."

Callie laughs, slipping off her shoes. "Welcome to Hollywood. The studio insists on it. Part of the premiere package."

I follow her through the living room, past a dining area that could seat twelve, and into the master bedroom. A massive bed dominates the space, draped in pristine white linens. Several garment bags hang on a rack by the wall, alongside stacks of boxes with names I vaguely recognize from magazines and commercials.

"Those are for you," she says, nodding toward three of the garment bags. "And those boxes should have shoes, accessories, all that."

I approach cautiously. Unzipping the first bag reveals a tuxedo that probably costs more than my mountainside property. I check the label: *Armani*. There's another bag with what looks like a more casual suit, and a third with various shirts and pants.

"How much did all of this cost?" I ask, unable to keep the edge from my voice. *Too fuckin' much for clothes*, is what I'm guessing.

She wraps her arms around my waist from behind. "It's part of the deal. The designers loan clothes in exchange for the publicity of having someone wear them on the red carpet."

"But I'm just security."

She rests her cheek against my back. "You're with me. That's enough for them."

I turn in her arms, studying her face. There's a tension around her eyes that wasn't there on the way here. "You doing okay?"

"Tired," she says. "And missing Hulk already."

"He's probably getting spoiled by my niece as we speak."

Her smile is small but genuine. "I hope so."

I brush a strand of hair from her face and lean in for a kiss. Her lips part under mine, soft and yielding. The familiar taste of her grounds me, reminding me that despite the unfamiliar surroundings, some things remain constant—the way she sighs into my mouth, the gentle press of her body against mine. *Her*.

She steps back, glancing toward an open door leading to what appears to be the bathroom. "I'm going to take a shower, wash off the travel."

I nod, letting her slip out of my arms and stare uncomfortably at the items before me. Not sure what to do with myself. Behind me, the bathroom door closes, then opens again.

"Beau?"

I glance over my shoulder. Callie's standing in the doorway, an invitation in her eyes. "This shower is pretty big," she says. A smile plays on her fuck-me lips. "I might need someone to watch my back..."

My cock thickens at the very thought of her asking me—wanting *me*. Three weeks we've been together, and my desire for her hasn't diminished at all. If anything, it's grown stronger with every second I'm with her.

I cross the room in a few strides, following her into a bathroom that's as big as her living room in Whitetail. White marble everywhere, a shower enclosure to fit five people with two showerheads, and a tub that could classify as a small pool.

She's already turning on the shower, steam beginning to rise. She turns to me, fingers slipping under the straps of her dress and shimmying it down her chest, waist, hips, thighs—before pooling at her feet. She steps out of it, wearing only a thin scrap of fabric between her thighs. *Fuck.*

My mouth goes dry at the sight of her naked, surrounded by this amount of luxury. The late afternoon California sun streams through frosted windows and catches her hair in a honey glow.

"You're overdressed," she points out with a smile, sliding her panties down her legs.

My cock weeps as she steps backward into the shower and the water that falls over her breasts, causing her nipples to perk.

I don't need to be told twice. I strip quickly, my clothes falling to the floor as I follow her under the spray. The water pressure is perfect, hot streams hitting my shoulders and easing the tension in my knee from the flight.

Callie presses against me, her skin slick and warm. "Hi," she says, looking up at me with those eyes that see right through me.

"Hi yourself," I murmur, before capturing her mouth with mine.

The kiss deepens immediately, urgent and hungry. She slides her hands up my chest and into my hair, pulling me closer. I press her against the cool tile wall, one hand braced above her head, the other trailing down her side to grip her hip.

"I missed you," she whispers against my lips.

"I haven't gone anywhere."

"No, but since we landed, you've been..." She looks away briefly, her cheeks turning a shade of pink. "Present but distant. Like you're on duty."

She's not wrong. I've been in assessment mode since we touched down. Knowing she wants me here as a means of protection—backup, as she calls it—has me scanning for threats, cataloging exits. She may have invited me to keep her safe, but every bone in me would have told me to do so regardless. "I'm right here, sweetheart," I say, pressing my forehead to hers. "I'm with you."

Her fingers trace the scar on my shoulder, then lower to wrap around my already hard cock. "I can tell," she says with a wicked smile.

My breath catches when she strokes me, her grip firm and sure. Then she sinks to her knees on the tile floor, looking up at me through wet lashes. "Callie—" I start, but the words die in my throat as her tongue laps at the head of my cock and her lips close around me.

The sight of her on her knees, taking me into her mouth, nearly undoes me. I keep one hand braced against the wall, the other tangling in her wet hair. She works me with her tongue, swirling around the head before she sucks me deeper, hollowing her cheeks with each slow, torturous pull.

When she looks up at me, holding my gaze as she takes me to the back of her throat, I have to grit my teeth to maintain control. Her hands aren't idle either—one grips the base of my shaft, working in tandem with her mouth, while the other cups and gently squeezes my balls, adding a layer of sensation that makes my thighs tense and a moan rip from my throat.

"Fuuuck," I groan as she takes me deeper. The hot water streams down my back while her mouth creates a different kind of heat altogether.

She pulls back slightly. "That's the idea," she says, breathless, verging on a moan of her own. "I want you to fuck me, Beau. Hard and fast."

The raw need in her voice tells me all I need to know. I haul her up and off the floor, pinning her against the wall. Her legs wrap around my waist and I can *feel* how wet she is against my stomach—her pussy dragging against me.

"Like this?" I ask, lowering her into position, lining the head of my cock at her entrance.

"Yes," she gasps. "Please."

I push into her in one smooth thrust and waste no time in pulling out, only to slam back into her. The angle is perfect, allowing me to go deep while supporting her weight against the wall. Her nails dig into my shoulders as I grip her hips. I set a pounding rhythm that's exactly what she asked for: hard and fast.

"God, yes," she moans, her head falling back against the tile.

The wet slap of our bodies coming together echoes around us. I drive into her, my grip on her thighs tight enough to leave marks. The thought sends a possessive pulse through my cock. "Look at me," I demand, needing to see her eyes.

She does, her gaze locking with mine as I thrust into her. The connection is electric, intimate. She starts to tighten around me, her breath becoming erratic. "Beau," she whimpers, her thighs trembling, her walls pulsing.

"I've got you, baby. I've always got you."

She cries out, her body clenching around mine as her orgasm hits. The feel of her coating my cock pushes me over the edge, and I follow her, burying my face in her neck as my release tears through me. *God, so fucking good.*

For a moment, we stay locked together, until I finally ease her down, making sure she's steady before reaching for the hotel-provided soap, one hand never leaving the curve of her hip.

Wild dogs couldn't tear me away from her.

She looks up at me, her expression dazed and soft. I pull her close, water streaming over us. We're silent as we wash each other slowly, taking our time. When we finally step out of the shower, it's nearing dinner and I'm starving.

Say what you will about sushi and the price of it, the shit isn't filling in the slightest.

I expect Callie to want to go out on the town, maybe catch dinner at another fancy restaurant, but she doesn't. And given what I know about her, I kick myself for not knowing better. We opt to order room service and she giggles incessantly at my massive order of steak and several sides we plan to share.

When it arrives, we lie in bed in our underwear and watch the first short horror film she ever made, *Blood Camp: S'mores and Slaughter*, on her laptop.

"You weren't kidding about the blood," I say around a mouthful of perfectly cooked ribeye. The screen shows a teenage counselor getting decapitated with what looks like fishing line, blood spraying in an improbable arc. "Is that corn syrup?"

"Corn syrup, food coloring, and chocolate sauce," she confirms, stealing a roasted potato from my plate. "My special recipe. We shot this senior year on a budget of exactly seventy-five dollars."

I'm impressed. "It looks professional."

"Thank you," she says, beaming with pride. "I was lucky enough to find actors willing to work for pizza and Pop Rocks."

As the movie plays, I study her more than the screen. She's relaxed in a way I haven't seen since the first night we spent together talking on her couch. Curled beside me in nothing but panties and my T-shirt, her hair still damp from our shower, this is the Callie I know—the one who'd rather watch horror movies in bed than parade around at fancy events and restaurants. I'm starting to see the conflict of interest here with her career.

She loves what she does.

But she doesn't love everything that comes with it.

"Did you act in any of your films?" I ask as the credits roll, showing a surprisingly short list of names for the twenty-three-minute movie.

She wrinkles her nose. "A few. I was usually behind the camera, but sometimes we'd run out of actors or someone would bail, and I'd have to step in."

"I want to see those," I say, setting my empty plate on the nightstand.

Her cheeks flush. "Oh, god no. They're embarrassing."

"All the more reason." I reach for the laptop, pulling it closer. "Come on, show me. I want to see everything you've made before you made it big."

She smiles, unable to hide her pleasure at my interest. "Fine. But you don't get to laugh at my terrible acting."

"No promises."

Her laugh has me grinning.

"After this, we should watch the first two in the trilogy," she says. "I'd hate to spoil the ending for you at the premiere. Oh, and I did play one of the early victims in the first movie."

I raise a brow. "You starred in one of your blockbusters?"

"It was fifteen minutes max," she says smoothly while pulling up another video, this one titled: *Nightmare Office: Deadline.* "In this one, I play the secretary who gets possessed by the ghost living in the copy machine."

"Naturally." I chuckle, bringing her against my side.

As the film begins, I'm struck by the strange twist of fate that brought us together—a stray bullet and a strong determination to keep the world at arm's length.

Now, I'm falling. Hard. Fast. With no end in sight.

"You're staring at me instead of the movie," she murmurs without looking away from the screen.

"Better view," I reply.

She turns to me then, her expression soft in the blue light of the laptop. "Thank you for coming with me," she says quietly. "I know this isn't your scene at all."

I brush my thumb across her cheek. "I'd follow you anywhere, sweetheart. Even into a ghost-possessed copy machine."

She laughs, the sound captivating. "Good to know you don't have limits."

I pull her closer for a kiss, the movie forgotten. This might be another world, full of expectations I can't begin to understand, but she's still the same woman who stole my heart in my hometown.

And for the next two weeks, I'll make damn sure nothing and no one hurts her.

Twenty-Two.

Beau

Callie twists her hands together in her lap, her eyes closed as the makeup artist does her thing.

I lean against the wall of the green room, arms crossed, watching the controlled chaos unfold around her. Six people hover in her orbit—makeup artist, hair stylist, wardrobe assistant, the production assistant, Ellen, and someone who keeps offering water no one asked for.

"Five minutes," Ellen announces, her attention split between her tablet and Callie. She's exactly what I expected—efficient, polished, mentally juggling seventeen tasks at once. "They're getting Jack mic'd up now."

I've been briefed on Jack Turner—lead actor, up-and-coming Hollywood golden boy, three blockbusters in the last year alone.

The way Ellen said his name, slightly hushed like it might summon him, tells me everything I need to know.

"And we're absolutely *not* discussing the Vanity Fair piece," Ellen continues, scrolling through her tablet. "I've made that clear to Monica, but if she tries to pivot there, just redirect to the film's themes."

Callie nods slightly, careful not to disturb the makeup brush sweeping across her cheekbones. "What about the screenplay nomination rumors?"

"Fair game, but downplay expectations. 'Too early to speculate' is your line."

My phone buzzes with a text from Duke—a video of Hulk playing with Olivia. I move closer to Callie, showing her the screen. Her entire face transforms, tension melting away as she watches the clip of her dog gently playing tug-of-war with the little girl.

"Aw," she coos softly.

Ellen clears her throat. "Two minutes, Callie. Let's go over the talking points for the creative process questions one more time."

I step back, tucking my phone in my pocket and resuming my position against the wall as Ellen rapid-fires potential questions and Callie's suggested responses.

It's like watching someone prepare for combat, but with words instead of weapons.

The door swings open without a knock. A man strides in—tall, tan, the kind of teeth that can't possibly be real. Jack Turner.

"Callie," he exclaims, arms spread wide as if he expects her to leap into his arms. I already don't like him. "The genius herself! Ready to make horror movie history?"

Callie stands, a professional smile replacing her genuine one from moments ago. "Jack, hi—" Before she can finish, he's embracing her, lifting her slightly off the ground in a bear hug that lasts several seconds too long by my estimation.

When he sets her down, his hands linger on her waist.

My jaw ticks.

"You look amazing," he says, gaze scanning her appreciatively. "As always." He winks.

Definitely don't like him.

"Thank you," she says, taking a subtle step back.

Jack's gaze finally registers my presence. His brows lift slightly, assessing me as I am him.

"Oh, Jack, this is Beau. He's my—"

"So listen, I was thinking after this wraps, we should grab dinner, catch up properly. It's been what, six months? I've missed our little chats," he says, his attention solely on her. I note how his hand has somehow found its way to the small of Callie's back.

The makeup artist returns, forcing Jack to step back as she applies a final touch to Callie's lips. I catch my girl's eye in the mirror, a silent communication passing between us.

Boyfriend.

That's what she wanted to announce to Jack.

"Actually, I have plans tonight," she says coolly. "But I'll see you at the premiere."

"Places, everyone!" a production assistant calls from the doorway.

Jack leans in, his lips brushing Callie's ear as he whispers something that makes her smile tighten. As they walk toward the door, his hand drifts lower than appropriate on her back for a split second before she casually shifts away.

I fight not to force my way between them and stay back a reasonable distance.

Ellen falls into step beside me as we follow them. "You're doing great," she says quietly. "Just remember—"

"Stay out of the shot, maintain sight lines, no visible reactions," I recite. "I got it."

She gives me an appraising look. "Good."

We enter the interview set—a minimal arrangement of modern chairs against a backdrop featuring the film's poster. Monica, the interviewer, is already seated, reviewing notes. Callie and Jack are directed to their marks, positioning them closer together than I would deem necessary.

I take my position off-camera within Callie's line of sight. From here, I can watch without being watched, which suits me fine.

"And we're rolling in three, two..." The producer points silently, and Monica's professional smile activates.

"I'm here today with writer and director Callie Ryan and star Jack Turner of the highly anticipated thriller and trilogy finale,

The Devil's Lake: Final Descent, in theaters this Friday. Callie, Jack, thank you both for being here."

The interview starts smoothly enough—questions about the film's development, Jack's preparation for his role, Callie's vision as creator and director. Callie transforms before my eyes, becoming more animated, more confident as she discusses her work. This is her element, and despite my general distaste for the Hollywood machine, I can't help but admire the joy on her face at this moment.

"Now, Callie," Monica pivots after about ten minutes, "your move to Montana earlier this year sparked quite a bit of industry speculation. Some suggested it was a creative retreat, others wondered if you were stepping back from directing altogether. Can you tell us what prompted the change?"

Callie's smile doesn't falter, but her hands tighten in her lap. "I needed a change of perspective to really see clearly. Montana offered me space to focus on what matters in my work."

"And what a focused creator she is," Jack interjects, placing his hand on Callie's knee. She flinches and I quell the urge to move. My fists ball at my sides. "The character development in this final act is what really sold me on the project."

Monica's eyes track the gesture, a slight smile playing at her lips. "Speaking of selling points, there have been rumors circulating about a special chemistry between the two of you during filming. Any truth to the whispers?"

Jack laughs, his hand still on Callie's knee. "Callie's brilliant, beautiful, and completely intimidating as a director. Any actor would be lucky to work with her—or be with her."

Callie shifts subtly, dislodging his hand. "Jack and I have a wonderful professional relationship," she says smoothly.

"Just professional?" Monica presses. "Because there were some rather cozy photos from the wrap party that suggested otherwise."

My jaw tightens, though I maintain my neutral expression. This wasn't on Ellen's approved question list, given the way she's suddenly alert standing beside me.

"Photos can be misleading," Callie says with a light laugh. "Especially when taken out of context at the end of an emotionally charged production period. Jack and I are colleagues and friends, nothing more."

"Not for lack of trying on my part," Jack adds with a wink that sets my teeth on edge.

Monica turns toward the camera. "You heard it here first, folks—officially just friends, but the door seems at least *slightly* ajar." The host chuckles.

"I have a boyfriend," Callie blurts, taking control of the rumor even now being spread. Her cheeks flush ever so slightly beneath her makeup.

My pulse jumps.

Monica's eyes widen with delight, her posture shifting forward like a predator sensing weakness. "Well, this *is* breaking news! The notoriously private Callie Ryan has a boyfriend." She turns to

Jack, whose smile has frozen in place. "Jack, did you know about this development?"

The camera pans to capture his reaction, and I can practically *see* the calculations happening behind his eyes. Attempting to appear supportive while salvaging his ego.

"This is the first I'm hearing of it," Jack says with practiced charm that doesn't match his posture. "Whoever he is, he's a lucky man."

Damn right I am.

Monica swivels back to Callie, not about to let this unexpected gold mine slip away. "So, tell us about this mystery man. Is he in the industry? How did you meet? And most importantly—will we be seeing him on the red carpet at the premiere?"

Ellen frantically makes a cutting motion off-camera, trying to redirect the interview to safer territory. But Monica isn't about to be deterred.

Callie recovers quickly, professional mask sliding back into place. "He'll be with me at the premiere, yes," she says. "But I'd really prefer to keep my personal life private. What I can tell you is that he's been incredibly supportive of my work and has seen every minute of film I've ever produced."

"A supportive partner is so important in this industry," Monica agrees, clearly not finished. "And where did you two meet? Was it on set?"

"Actually, we met in Montana," Callie offers, deciding to give just enough to satisfy the bloodthirsty host without revealing too much. "He's from there."

"Montana!" Monica's perfectly shaped eyebrows rise. "So not industry at all. How refreshing."

Multiple pairs of eyes flick to me momentarily before returning to the interview. My face remains impassive, though I'm hyperaware of every muscle in my body, every slam of my heart against my ribcage.

She's telling the whole world that she's taken—that she's *mine*.

Callie's smile is stunning. "It really is. He's amazing."

Jack shifts in his seat, his body language betraying his discomfort at being sidelined.

"Well, we can't wait to meet him," Monica says, finally pivoting. "Now, speaking of building beautiful things, let's talk about the world-building you set in the first film, *The Devil's Lake: Beneath the Surface...*"

The interview continues for another five minutes, but the energy has shifted. Jack makes valiant attempts to reclaim the spotlight, but there's a new dynamic at play. Callie answers questions about the film with renewed confidence, while Monica occasionally glances toward me with curiosity.

When the producer finally calls, "That's a wrap, folks!" Callie's shoulders relax.

"Thank you both so much," Monica says, removing her microphone. Off-camera, her demeanor softens into something more genuine. "Seriously, Callie, I can't wait to see the film. The early buzz is phenomenal."

"Thanks, Monica," she says, standing and handing her mic to a waiting technician.

Jack rises beside her, leaning in close as I approach. "Boyfriend, huh? You could have mentioned that earlier," he says, voice low but audible enough.

"It didn't seem relevant to the interview," Callie replies coolly.

"Everything's relevant in these situations," he counters. "Makes me look like an ass."

Monica, pretending not to eavesdrop while absorbing every word, chooses this moment to extend her hand to me, now standing beside Callie. "I don't think we've been formally introduced. Monica Chen."

"Beau Montgomery," I reply, taking her hand briefly.

"Bodyguard, right?" Her eyes are shrewd, assessing. "Or...more than security?"

Before I can respond, Ellen materializes between us. "I'm so sorry to interrupt, but we're on a very tight schedule. Callie, we need to move to the next appointment."

"Of course," Callie says, moving smoothly to my side. "Monica, Jack, thank you both."

Ellen efficiently leads us toward the exit, creating a buffer between Callie and any further questions. It's only when we're safely in the hallway, doors closed behind us, that Ellen lets out a long breath. "Well, that wasn't in the talking points."

"I'm sorry," Callie says, glancing between her assistant and me. "It just came out."

"Don't apologize," Ellen says. "It was authentic, and it completely redirected the Jack narrative that you've been trying to get away from for *years*. 'Reclusive director finds love in Montana' is a much better headline than recycled on-set romance rumors."

Callie looks at me, uncertainty in her eyes. "Are you okay with this? I didn't mean to put you in the spotlight."

I consider my answer carefully, aware of Ellen pretending to check her tablet while listening. "It's not my world," I admit. "But you are."

The tension in Callie's expression dissolves into a small, intimate smile.

Ellen clears her throat. "If you two are done being adorable, we do have a fitting to get to."

As we walk down the hallway, Callie's hand stays firmly in mine. I'm hyperaware of the curious glances from staff and guests. In Montana, she's just Callie, the new girl in town renting a cabin on the mountain. Here, she's someone people recognize, someone they whisper about as we pass.

Outside in the California sunshine, I realize something. I may hate the cameras, the invasive questions, the Jack Turners of this world with their easy smiles and wandering hands—but Callie?

I love her.

Twenty-Three.

Callie

"I CAN'T BELIEVE YOU said that," Shea gasps, staring at her phone with rapt attention as the interview plays a second time. It's been uploaded for all of thirty minutes and several entertainment news outlets have already picked up the story as if it were their own. "Jack looks *pissed*."

Beau snorts from his spot on the sofa in our hotel room, watching with smug appreciation as Shea's fashion intern helps me into my dress for a final fitting.

I stick my tongue out at him and he laughs.

"It just came out," I explain, raising my arms as the intern—a serious-faced girl named Maya—works on pinning the final adjustments to the sides of the gown. "Jack was being so..."

"Handsy?" Shea supplies. "Presumptuous? His usual self?"

"All of the above." I rotate slowly as directed. The dusty pink fabric lined with sequins catches the light and glitters around us. "Monica wasn't on the approved question list with that one. Ellen nearly had a stroke."

"Well, this article is calling it 'the most authentic moment in press junket history,' so there's that," Shea says, still scrolling. "Oh, and People wants an exclusive on your *Montana romance*—Ellen's already fielding requests."

I glance at Beau, trying to gauge his reaction. He seems unbothered, watching the proceedings with the same calm attentiveness he brings to everything. But there's something in his eyes when they meet mine. Quiet pride, maybe?

"No exclusives," I say firmly. "Our relationship isn't a publicity stunt."

"Smart," Shea nods. "Keep them guessing. The mystery boyfriend angle will generate more buzz anyway."

Beau raises a brow. "Mystery boyfriend?"

"That's what they're calling you," Shea informs him with delight. "My current favorite is that you're a rugged Montana rancher who tamed Hollywood's most private director."

I can't help but laugh at Beau's expression. So serious.

"I don't ranch," he points out dryly.

"Details." Shea waves dismissively, a hint of glee in her voice at being able to tease Beau. He gets riled up so easily. And she's taking full advantage. "The narrative is what matters. And this narrative is gold, especially compared to the tired 'director-actor on-set romance' they were trying to push with Jack."

The intern finishes her pinning and steps back. "All done. If you can take it off carefully, I'll have these minor alterations finished by tonight."

"It's perfect," I say, admiring the dress in the full-length mirror. The color complements my hair and skin tone, and the cut is both elegant and comfortable—a rare combination in an evening gown.

My best friend beams at the sight of me. "Gorgeous."

A knock at the door interrupts us. Beau is up and alert, walking to the door to check the peephole before I can even turn around.

"It's your father," he tells me.

My brow furrows. I haven't talked to him since we landed on Sunday. It's Tuesday.

Beau opens the door, and my father steps in, looking out of place and unfazed in his department-issued attire. "Callie," he says, his weathered face breaking into a smile when he sees me. "Department needs me tomorrow for a task force meeting, so I wanted to wish you luck in person before the show."

I carefully maneuver in my half-pinned dress to hug him. "I'm glad you stopped by."

He holds me at arm's length, taking in the dress with genuine admiration. "You look great, honey," he says softly for only me to hear. "Just like your mother in that color."

The comparison to my mom catches me off guard, a lump forming in my throat. She died in a car accident when I was an infant. And with few pictures and Dad rarely wanting to talk about her... This moment feels special. "Thanks, Dad."

He clears his throat, the moment passing as quickly as it came. Typical Matthew Ryan. "Shea," he acknowledges with a nod.

"Hey, Matt," Shea replies with the easy familiarity of someone who knows his aloof demeanor is never personal.

Dad turns his attention to Beau, who's been standing quietly near the door. "Montgomery," he says, extending his hand. "Good to see you again."

"Sir," Beau replies, shaking his hand firmly.

"You looked after her yesterday at that interview thing?" Dad asks, his tone casual, but his eyes sharp.

"Yes, sir," Beau says simply.

Dad nods, satisfied. "Mind if we have a chat downstairs?"

My stomach tightens instinctively. Dad doesn't 'chat' with people. He interrogates them. "Dad, Beau doesn't need the third degree—"

"It's fine." Beau gives me a reassuring nod.

Dad turns to me. "Won't keep him long."

I narrow my eyes at him. "Be nice."

"Always am," he says with the innocent expression that never fooled me, even as a kid.

Maya clears her throat. "Miss Ryan, we should get you out of the dress before the pins shift."

"Right," I say, reluctantly turning away. "You two go ahead. But Dad—"

"I know, I know," he says, heading for the door. "No threats, best behavior."

"That's not reassuring!" I call after them as the door closes.

Shea waits approximately two seconds before bursting into laughter. "Your face right now is priceless."

"It's not funny," I grumble as Maya helps me carefully step out of the dress. My mind swims with what they could possibly need to talk about. Of course, the only thing that comes to mind is...me. "You know how he is."

"Beau can handle himself," Shea says confidently. "That man radiates 'can handle himself' energy."

Once I'm back in a cozy white robe, Maya leaves with the dress, promising to return it by this evening. As the door closes behind her, Shea plops onto the sofa beside me, tucking her feet beneath her. "So," she says, her expression turning serious. "Now that we're alone—what's really going on with you two?"

"What do you mean?"

"Come on, Cals. You've been vague about your relationship for months. Then *boom!* he's your boyfriend on national television. That's a big step for someone who's been keeping her dating life under lock and key since college."

I sigh, knowing she's right. "We've been serious for the last three weeks. It just sort of...happened."

"The best things usually do," she says with a smile. "But are you happy? Because I've been watching you two and I've never seen you like this with anyone."

"Like what?"

"Completely yourself," she says simply. "No filters, no walls, no director-mode armor. You look at him like he's your safe place." Adding coyly, "Similar to how you look at me, actually."

I laugh, but her observation hits closer to home than I expected. "He is," I admit quietly.

"So it's serious?" Shea asks, her eyes soft with understanding.

I nod, a little surprised at how easy the admission is. "Yeah. It is."

"And the L-word?"

"We haven't said it," I confess. "But I think...it's there."

Shea squeals, bouncing in her seat. "I knew it! The way he looks at you when you're not watching—that man is *gone* for you."

"Really?" I can't help the hopeful note in my voice. Does he? Could he really...love me already? It's fast. *Really* fast. But it feels right. So damn right it's hard to comprehend.

"Absolutely. And I have to say, as your best friend who's seen you through some truly questionable choices—" She gives me a pointed look. "—I approve. One hundred percent."

I smile, laughing with watery eyes. "You do?"

"He's solid, Cal. Grounded. And he clearly adores you without trying to use your success as a stepping stone. Plus," she adds with a grin, "he was ready to murder Jack yesterday for touching your *knee* of all things. That's both terrifying and hot."

I laugh, feeling a weight lift that I didn't realize I was carrying. "I wasn't sure if... I mean, this world is so different from his."

"Maybe that's exactly what you need," Shea suggests. "Someone who sees past all this—" She gestures around the luxury hotel room. "—to the *real* you."

The real me. The me that's not sidelined by fear and paranoia. The me that loves movies and writing and directing. "I like her better, I think."

"I like her, too," Shea says, her expression turning slightly mischievous. "Also, the sex must be *incredible*, because you're practically glowing."

"Shea!"

"What? I'm simply saying what we're all thinking. That man looks like he knows what he's doing."

My cheeks heat. "I'm not discussing this with you...right now." She knows I tell her everything, but not when Beau or my dad could walk in at any moment.

"Your blush tells me everything I need to know," she says triumphantly. Then, more seriously, "I'm happy for you, Cals. Really."

"Thanks," I say, feeling emotional. "Your opinion means a lot to me."

"I know," she says with exaggerated confidence that makes me laugh. "Now, tell me honestly, what do they feed these men out there? Are they all built like *that*?"

As I fill her in on what I've seen 'men-wise' in Whitetail, I find myself wondering what's going on downstairs. Strangely, I'm not worried. Something tells me that whatever interrogation tactics my father is employing, Beau can hold his own.

I hope.

Twenty-Four.

Beau

I STEP INTO THE private elevator alongside Callie's father. He presses the button for the lobby and our descent begins. I assume this is about the interview and my relationship with his daughter, but I'm not worried. Though, I wouldn't doubt if he *wants* me to be.

The silence stretches between us, neither of us speaking as the floors tick by. I've faced far worse overseas and survived a bullet to the knee. One protective father isn't going to rattle me, even if he is a cop.

"Bar's this way," he says as we exit into the marble-floored lobby.

He moves with the same alertness I recognize from men who've spent their lives assessing threats. I follow him through the lobby to a dimly lit bar with leather chairs and dark wood. It's early enough that the place is nearly empty. We take a seat at a corner table, both of us instinctively positioning ourselves to see the entrance.

A server appears, and Matt orders a scotch, neat. I ask for the same.

"Been a while since we met in Montana," he says once the server leaves. "Few weeks?"

"Three."

He nods, studying me. "So, things have changed."

It's not a question, but I answer anyway. "Yes, sir."

"When?"

"About three weeks ago," I say, deciding honesty is the only appropriate approach.

His jaw tightens, but he doesn't seem surprised. "You know," he says, setting his glass down, "when Callie moved to Montana, I thought she was running away. Hiding from her success and everything that transpired because of it."

I recognize his technique—sharing something to get me to share more. Fortunately for him, he's also not wrong. "She was," I acknowledge. "At first."

"And now?"

"She's found her footing." I take a drink, the scotch burning down my throat. Part of me realizes he should be having this conversation with his daughter, but I humor him anyway. "She never stopped working—editing, writing. Montana gave her the space to do it without the pressure."

Matt studies me over his glass. "You know about what happened before? The reason she left LA?"

"Yes." I don't elaborate. I know enough to know her fear is warranted and that he's the reason she has Hulk in the first place. To be everywhere he couldn't be. Now, I'm here instead of Hulk.

"And that interview yesterday? Calling you her boyfriend on national television?"

There it is. "That wasn't planned."

He leans back in his chair. "My daughter doesn't do impulsive."

"She's still careful," I assure him. "Just not afraid anymore."

My words land differently than I expect. His expression softens minutely, something like relief flickering across his features before his stonewalled expression returns. "I looked you up," he says, changing tactics. "Army Special Forces. Two tours. Honorable discharge after taking a bullet in Afghanistan."

I nod, unsurprised. I'd have done the same in his position.

"What are your intentions with my daughter, Montgomery?"

The directness of the question catches me on guard, and I appreciate it. No point dancing around what he really wants to know. "I care about her," I say. "I want her safe and happy. The rest is up to her."

"That's a politician's answer."

I meet his gaze. Firm and unwavering. "It's the truth."

Matthew's eyes narrow, assessing. "You're in love with her."

It's not a question, but my heart still kicks against my ribs at hearing someone else say it aloud. I haven't said those words to

Callie, but fuck, do I feel them. The last few days here with her have been the highlight of my year. She drowns out everything that's changed. Everything I thought I'd lost—my career, my future. She's taken the hardest time in my life and made it into something worth waking up for. Her.

"Yes," I admit.

"And does she know that?"

I take another sip of my drink. "Not yet."

He huffs, his gaze suspicious. He leans forward, all pretense of casual conversation gone. "Let me be clear, Montgomery. Callie is all I have in this world. After her mother died, it was us against the world. It has always been *us*. She's dealt with enough shit already—the stalking, the threats, the industry assholes who continue to try to use her or control her. I won't stand by and watch her get hurt again."

"With all due respect, sir," I say, keeping my voice even. "I'm not in the business of hurting people I love."

"No one ever is until they do." His eyes are hard, but there's something vulnerable behind them—the worry of a father who's seen his daughter hurt one too many times. "This industry she's in, the spotlight; it changes people. Adds pressure. I've seen it destroy stronger couples than a three-week fling."

My jaw tightens. If he's trying to push me for a reaction, he's getting damn close. "This isn't a fling."

"Prove it," he challenges.

"I don't have to prove anything to you," I snap, willing myself to dial it back a peg. Or two. I need to remember this is my girl's *father*. "Only to Callie. And I do that every day by being there for her, respecting her, and having her back."

Matt stares at me for a long moment, then does something unexpected—he smiles. It's small, but genuine. "Good answer," he says, raising his glass in my direction. "That's exactly what I wanted to hear."

I feel like I just passed some test I didn't know I was taking. "So that's what this was then, a test?"

"More or less." He finishes his scotch. "Had to be sure you weren't just along for the ride on her success. Or worse, another controlling prick who thinks he knows what's best for her."

"I'm neither." Though my gripe on hiking apparel does come to mind.

"I believe you." He signals the server for another round. "Now, tell me more about this cabin you're building. Callie sends pictures, but she's not great with the technical details."

The abrupt shift in conversation throws me for a moment, but I go with it, describing the progress on the cabin, the design elements, and the timeline for completion. Matthew listens with genuine interest, asking questions that show he knows more about construction than I would have guessed.

As our second drinks arrive, he says, "You know, her mother would have liked you."

"Callie doesn't talk about her much."

"No, she wouldn't." He stares down at his glass. "Callie was just a baby when she died. Car accident. Drunk driver hit her head-on coming home from the grocery store." He takes a breath. "I wasn't great at talking about her afterward."

I'm not sure why he's telling me this, but I listen, recognizing the importance of what he's sharing as well as this chat for him.

He clears his throat and checks his watch. Appearing as though the direction of the conversation has taken him somewhere he doesn't like being. "I should head out."

We finish our drinks and Matthew's demeanor shifts, becoming less interrogator and more of a father concerned for his daughter. "One more thing," he says as we stand to leave. "That Jack Turner guy—"

"Won't be a problem," I say, and damn sure mean it.

A flash of understanding passes between us. "Good." He extends his hand. "You have my blessing. Take care of her, Montgomery."

The double meaning in his strategically chosen words isn't lost on me.

I shake his hand firmly. "I will."

The sun hangs low over the Pacific, painting the sky in shades I never see in Montana—vibrant oranges blending into pinks against a backdrop of pale blue. It's different from our sunsets back home, where the mountains catch the last light in sharp, dramatic silhouettes, and the colors are deeper, more saturated against the vast open sky.

Here, the horizon is a straight line where ocean meets atmosphere, endless and somehow more expansive and confined than the mountain ranges I'm used to. The air feels different, too—heavy with salt and moisture instead of crisp pine and fresh air.

Callie walks beside me, her sandals dangling from one hand, a frozen yogurt cup in the other. After the meeting with her father and an afternoon of final preparations for tomorrow's premiere, she suggested we go for a walk with a smile that made it impossible to say no to her.

She led the way to a small stretch of beach accessed through a narrow path between two private properties. "It's my old film professor's house," she explained as we squeezed through. "He lets former students use his beach access. Much quieter than the public beaches."

Apart from a couple walking a dog in the distance, we have the shore to ourselves. The sand is still warm beneath my bare feet despite the setting sun, and the gentle rhythm of waves provides a soothing soundtrack. It's a sound one could get used to.

"Penny for your thoughts?" Callie asks, spooning the last of her strawberry frozen yogurt into her mouth.

"Noting the differences," I reply, finishing my vanilla yogurt with a swirl of caramel. "Between here and home."

Her eyes soften at the word *home*. "Good or bad?" she asks, tossing her empty cup into a nearby trash can.

"Just different," I say, disposing of mine as well. "The sunset here is...soft. Back home, it's sharper, more defined by the mountains."

She nods, understanding what I'm trying to say better than I do myself. "I miss that clarity sometimes. Everything here has a haze to it—the air, the light, even the conversations."

We walk in comfortable silence for a while, close enough that our arms brush occasionally. The receding tide has left the sand wet and firm, easier to walk on than the loose, dry sand higher up.

"How was your talk with my dad?" she finally asks, the question I've been expecting since we left the hotel.

"Good," I grunt. "He's protective of you."

She rolls her eyes. "Did he threaten you?"

"Didn't have to." I smile to show I'm not bothered. "He cares about you. I respect that."

"What did you talk about?"

"You, mostly." I take her hand as we navigate around a piece of driftwood. "The cabin. Your mom a little bit."

She stares at me in surprise. "He talked about my mom?"

"Said she would have liked me," I tell her, watching her reaction. "Said you're a lot like her."

Her eyes grow misty, and she looks toward the ocean. "He never says that."

I squeeze her hand gently. "He also made it clear that if I hurt you, they'll never find my body."

That gets a laugh from her. "And what did you tell him?"

"That I have no intention of hurting you." I pause, wondering if this is the moment. It feels right, with the sunset casting golden light across her face, the waves providing a steady rhythm that no longer matches my heartbeat. "Ever."

She stops walking and faces me, her expression open and curious. "You sound pretty sure about that."

"I am." I tuck a wild, honey-colored curl behind her ear, marveling at how the sunset makes her skin glow. "More sure than I've been about anything in a long time."

Her breath catches. "Beau..."

"I love you, Callie," I say, voice low. My chest expands at how natural it feels to be telling her how I feel. Emotions, feelings—the whole lot of it is something I never saw the appeal in. Though I can't say I've felt this way about anyone before. She's the first woman I've said those three words to. "I know it hasn't been long, but it's the truth."

For a moment, she just stares at me, and I wonder if I've miscalculated, moved too fast.

Her face breaks into the most beautiful smile I've ever seen. "I love you, too," she whispers, rising on her tiptoes to press her lips to mine.

The kiss is soft, tender, tasting of strawberries and salt. When we part, her eyes are shining. I hold her close and keep her there against my chest, breathing in the scent of her mixed with ocean air. Beside us, the sun continues its descent, casting our shadows across the sand.

"Can I ask you a personal question?" she mumbles into me, her face turned to the setting sun.

I hum, my gaze cast over her head at the very same view. I place a kiss in her hair. "Shoot."

"Do you think you're the same person?" she asks softly. "You know, before you left."

The question is vague, but I know what she's asking without the details. *Am I the same person I was before I left for the military?* "There are plenty of men, women, who feel they come back different. That they've changed somehow."

She nods, listening.

"I never felt that," I confess, my arms tightening around her at the admission. "And either I'm lucky or...cold."

She peers up at me finally, her expression soft. "You're not cold."

The last time I saw Rhett flashes in my mind. How hard he was trying to talk to me and how hard I fought back to keep everyone at arm's length—or farther. "My family would disagree."

Her brow furrows, an edge of adorable defiance I've seen more than once in her eyes. "Then they don't know you like I do."

I huff a laugh. "Only you, sweetheart."

We head back, our footprints leaving parallel trails in the damp sand. The sun hangs low now, casting long shadows ahead of us as we walk toward the narrow path.

"Tell me something about Montana," she says, slipping her hand in mine as we walk. "What's your favorite thing about it?"

I think for a moment. *My favorite thing.* "There's this moment, just before sunrise, when the mountains are still dark, but the sky is beginning to lighten. Everything is perfectly still—no wind, no sound. It's like the whole world is holding its breath. Then, when the first light hits the highest peaks, it's like watching the earth wake up one ridge at a time."

"That's beautiful." She peers up at me, beaming. "You should write that down."

I chuckle. "Nah. That's your department."

She smiles, and we pause where the beach narrows, the water now painting ribbons of gold and crimson across the surface as we watch the last sliver of sun disappear below the horizon. Tomorrow will bring chaos—cameras and questions, politics and public scrutiny.

But right now, it's just us, the beach, and a few words that have changed everything.

I pull her close, and she comes willingly, fitting against me perfectly. As darkness settles over the beach, I hold tight to the woman who crashed into my carefully constructed solitude and turned it into something infinitely better—a life built for two.

Twenty-Five.

Callie

I BLOW OUT A breath and shake out my hands in front of me.

"How are you doing, Callie? Can I get you anything? Water, gum?" Ellen asks, a phone in each of her hands as she checks her meticulously set, by-the-minute schedule.

"I'm fine." The lie comes automatically. My heart is pounding so hard I can hear it in my ears alongside a familiar tightness in my chest that's threatening to overwhelm me.

We're in the back of the limo, moments away from pulling up to the theater. Outside the tinted windows waits a gauntlet of photographers, reporters, and fans—all eyes waiting for me and the cast to walk the red carpet.

I wish Hulk were here...

Beau grips my thigh from his spot beside me, a solid presence in his perfectly tailored tuxedo. I shift my focus to him. He's devastatingly handsome—the black suit emphasizes his broad shoulders and the crisp white shirt makes me want to crawl inside, rest my head on his juicy pecs, and never come out.

His gaze meets mine, steady and calm.

"Breathe," he says quietly, just for me. His thumb presses into my thigh, forcing me to focus. To listen.

I take a deep breath, my bare shoulders rising with the action. He doesn't smile or offer any words of encouragement. He doesn't have to. He simply holds my gaze and breathes with me. He rubs his thumb back and forth over my skin through the slit on my dress.

Last night on the beach feels like a dream now. His quiet confession of love, the peaceful sunset, the simplicity of the moment. It was perfect. This, however, the premiere, the cameras, the noise—not so much.

"Thirty seconds," Ellen announces, checking her phone. "Jack and the rest of the cast are already on the carpet. Studio executives are waiting to greet you at the entrance."

I take another deep breath. "How do I look?" I ask no one in particular.

The dusty pink, mermaid gown catches the light with every movement, thousands of hand-sewn sequins creating a subtle shimmer. It's elegant without being flashy, and the fabric is cool against my skin. My hair is pinned back, makeup done professionally.

Shea sits across from us in a stunning, golden gown of her own design and gives me an encouraging smile. "Absolutely perfect."

"Everyone knows the plan," Ellen reminds us all. "Beau stays with you as security. The press has been briefed not to ask personal questions, but be prepared for some to try anyway. Keep responses focused on the film."

The car slows, and my stomach drops as I catch sight of the crowd outside. It's ten times larger than I expected, with barricades holding back fans and photographers lined up three to four deep.

"Oh, god," I whisper.

Beau squeezes my hand. "I've got you."

I turn to him and blow out an anxious breath. Those three words steady me more than any breathing exercise could.

The car stops. Ellen exits first, then Shea, who turns to give me one last thumbs-up before disappearing into the flash of cameras. Then, it's our turn.

Beau steps out first, all military precision in his movements as he extends his hand to help me from the car. The moment my heels touch the red carpet, the noise hits me. A wall of shouted names, camera shutters, and the dull roar of the crowd.

"Callie! Callie, over here!"

"Miss Ryan, this way, please!"

"Here, here!"

"Callie, who are you wearing?"

Beau's hand rests on the small of my back, a reminder that I'm not alone. His presence behind me feels like a shield as I plaster on my practiced smile and begin to walk.

The first section is just photographers—no questions, just a flurry of flashes and shouted directions. I know the drill: pause every few feet, turn slightly, smile. Beau stays behind me but remains within reach. His face carefully neutral.

"You're doing great, sweetheart," he murmurs when I pause between photo spots.

I manage a genuine smile in response, and the cameras go wild, mistaking it for a posed shot.

The next section is the press line—television cameras and reporters with microphones, each allocated a few precious minutes. This is the part I dread most. It's like being trapped, stuck in a mud that no one will tug you out of until they've gotten theirs.

"Callie Ryan." The first reporter beams at me. "Congratulations on the film. How does it feel to be back after your hiatus?"

"Thank you," I say, the practiced answer coming easily. "It feels wonderful to share this film with audiences. The entire team has worked incredibly hard."

"And we understand this is the final part of the trilogy? Can you tell us what to expect from you next?"

I relax slightly, grateful for the focus on the creativity in my work. "*The Devil's Lake* trilogy had a layer of mystery I aim to pull from in my next screenplay. Think, psychological thriller that explores a hidden darkness beneath seemingly perfect individuals."

The interview continues smoothly, and I begin to find my rhythm. Beau remains a constant presence, his gaze scanning the crowd in a way that I desperately want to know what he thinks of all this. *Is it too much for him?*

Three interviews in, I spot Jack Turner farther down the carpet with a group of reporters. Our eyes meet briefly, and he makes his way toward me. "Callie," he calls, approaching with his trademark, camera-ready smile. "You look stunning."

"Thank you, Jack," I say, aware of the cameras swiveling to capture our interaction.

He leans in for an air kiss, his hand finding my waist in a gesture that looks friendly to observers, but feels possessive. Behind me, the heat of Beau creeps forward. My heart rate kicks up a notch.

"The reviews are already coming in," Jack says. "They're calling it your best work yet."

"It was a team effort," I deflect. *Just keep smiling.*

"Always so modest," he says with a laugh that's a touch too familiar. "We should take some photos together for the press. The director and her leading man."

Before I can respond, Ellen appears at my side. "Callie, the studio heads are waiting to speak with you," she says smoothly. "Jack, I believe Entertainment Tonight is looking for you at position five."

Jack beams, his chest and ego inflating in tandem. "Of course. Catch up at the after-party, Cal?"

"We'll see," I say noncommittally. "Enjoy the screening."

As he moves away, I mouth a silent *thank you* to Ellen, who gives me a subtle nod before guiding me toward the next interview.

The rest of the press line goes smoothly until we reach the final section, where fans have gathered behind barricades. My anxiety spikes again—the unpredictability of fan crowds has always been a trigger for me.

"You don't have to stop," Beau says quietly. "We can go straight inside."

I shake my head. "No, these people have been waiting for hours. I can do this."

I approach the barricade, smiling and signing the posters and photos thrust toward me. Most of the fans are respectful, excited to share their enthusiasm for my previous work.

"I loved *Midnight Echo*," one young woman gushes. "It inspired me to apply to film school!"

"That's wonderful," I tell her sincerely. "What's your name?"

"Amber," she says, beaming as I sign her DVD cover.

I'm just turning to the next fan when a commotion erupts farther down the line. A man vaults over the barricade, shoving past security and running straight toward me.

My heart drops to the pit of my stomach.

"Callie! Callie, I've been trying to reach you," he shouts, his eyes wild.

Time slows. My body freezes. The memory of another man, another crowd, another moment when control was ripped away from me surges to the surface. The panic rises, choking me, paralyzing my limbs.

But before I can fully process what's happening, Beau is there.

In one fluid motion, he steps between me and the approaching man, his stance protective. The security team converges, but it's Beau who makes first contact.

"That's far enough," he says, his voice calm but with an unmistakable authority that stops the man in his tracks.

I take a step closer to Beau, needing to touch him. To keep myself grounded. To breathe. My shaking hand finds his and the other rests on his lower back. *Breathe.*

"I just need to talk to her," the man insists, trying to look around Beau to me. "I sent scripts—dozens of them. She needs to read them. We're meant to work together!"

"Miss Ryan isn't accepting unsolicited materials," Beau replies evenly with an edge of heat that has my insides coiling. He doesn't move an inch. "You need to step back. *Now.*"

The security team reaches us, flanking the man who continues to protest as they roughly escort him back behind the barricade. Beau turns to me, his back to the cameras, creating a small pocket of privacy in the chaos. "You're all right, sweetheart," he says quietly. "Breathe with me."

I follow his lead, focusing on his steady gaze rather than the commotion around us. Ellen and Shea have rushed over, forming a protective circle around me. "We can go in through the side entrance," Ellen suggests. "Skip the rest of the line."

"No, I... Give me a minute," I say, still holding Beau's gaze like a lifeline. The panic is receding, slowly but surely. I inhale deeply. "I can do this."

Concern flashes across Beau's face. "Baby, you don't have to—"

"I do," I cut him off gently. I'm so tired of letting my success drown me rather than lift me. Fear is a tool, a means for survival. It's not meant to control me. Not forever. "I need to."

He studies me for a moment, then nods, understanding what this means to me. "I'm right here."

I smile, small but genuine. "I know." *You're the reason I'm still standing here.*

The security team has removed the man, and the crowd is watching anxiously. The mood shifted. If I leave now, this incident becomes the story—not the film, not all my hard work, but my fear. Another headline about Callie Ryan's breakdown.

I straighten my shoulders and turn to the crowd with a smile that costs me everything to maintain. "I'm so sorry about the interruption," I say to the waiting fans. "Where were we?"

A collective breath of relief seems to pass through the crowd. I sign a few more autographs, pose for a couple of selfies, then allow Ellen to guide me toward the theater entrance where the studio executives wait.

"Are you sure you're okay?" Shea whispers as we approach the doors.

"I will be," I tell her, and I mean it.

Inside the theater lobby, away from the cameras, I finally let myself lean against Beau for a moment. "Thank you," I murmur as his mass of muscle and warmth and everything that is *him* closes around me.

His arm circles my waist, securing me to him. "I'm proud of you," he says, voice low.

I peer up at him, his heated gaze staring down at me. "I couldn't have done it without you."

"Yes, you could have," he grumbles. "But I'm glad you didn't have to."

Ellen approaches with a water bottle and a concerned expression. "The incident has already hit social media, but our team is controlling the narrative—focusing on how professionally it was handled and how graciously you continued afterward."

"Good," I say, taking a sip of water. "What's next?"

"Brief remarks before the screening," she says, checking her second phone. "Then you can relax and watch the film. The hard part is over."

We both know that's not entirely true. The screening means sitting in darkness, surrounded by hundreds of people reacting to my work in real time. The after-party means hours of networking disguised as celebration. Then, as she mentioned, there's all the social media that will come over the next few weeks.

"Miss Ryan." One of the studio executives approaches, hand extended. "Remarkable job. The film is getting tremendous buzz already. The entire trilogy is, actually."

I slip into a professional blur of shaking hands and exchanging pleasantries with the line of executives and investors waiting to speak with me. Beau steps back to a respectful distance, but still close enough that his solid, unyielding presence grounds me.

As I'm ushered toward the theater entrance to give my opening remarks, I catch his eye one last time. He gives me a small nod that carries the weight of everything we've shared—petty arguments, helpless moments, sunsets, and three words that have changed everything.

I take a deep breath and step onto the stage, facing the audience gathered here to see my vision come to life. The lights are bright. The crowd quiet. Excitement radiates throughout the room. And I feel it, too.

"Thank you all for coming tonight," I begin, my voice steady with only a *slightly* shaky hand as I adjust the microphone stand in front of me. "Creating *The Devil's Lake* has been a heck of a journey for me. I faced a lot of fears and found strength in a few...unexpected places." I glance to my right at the man standing off stage with his hands clasped in front of him, as handsome and stoic as ever. He grins. "In the end, I found what I was looking for. My final piece. My home." I turn to the audience. "I'd like to thank the incredible cast and crew who poured their hearts into making this vision a reality. And finally, I want to thank someone who told me that sometimes, the bravest thing we can do isn't facing our fears, but allowing others to stand beside us when we do." My voice softens. "And that true strength comes from connection, not isolation."

The audience is silent in a way that tells me they're truly listening, not just waiting for the movie to begin. I smile and end with, "I hope this final chapter resonates with you tonight. I hope it reminds you that we all have depths worth exploring, fears worth facing, and connections worth fighting for. Thank you."

Applause washes over me as I step away from the mic. Beau offers me his hand when I walk down the side of the stage and into his arms. He pulls me in and kisses me as if we're the only two in the room.

His lips are warm and firm against mine, one hand cradling the back of my neck while the other rests possessively at my waist. I taste the faint hint of mint on his breath, relish the gentle scratch of his stubble against my skin. My body melts into his as the noise of the crowd fades to a distant hum and the lights lower for the film to begin.

"Nice speech," he whispers against my lips.

I smile, peppering his lips with mine. "Nice lipstick."

"Glad you like it," he says, smug. "Took me years to find the right one."

I raise a brow. "Oh, yeah?"

He slides his hands down the curve of my waist to settle low on my hips. "Yeah," he breathes, leaning in close. "She's perfect."

Twenty-Six.

Callie

My fingers dig into the sheets as Beau moves behind me, his powerful hands holding my hips in a vice grip. Each thrust sends jolts of pleasure coursing up my spine, wrenching moan after moan from my lips as he claims me completely.

"God, you feel incredible," he rasps, his voice a jagged growl of desire. "So damn perfect."

His words ignite my core. There's something about being back in Montana, in my bed—*our* bed where we're making up for lost time.

"Harder," I plead, pressing back against him, arching deeper into the mattress. "Please. Fuck me, Beau."

He responds immediately, his pace increasing as he slides one hand up my bare back to tangle in my hair, gripping it at the root. His gentle tug sends another spike of pleasure through me, heightening every sensation. I moan.

"You like that, don't you?" His voice is a seductive whisper, dark and velvety. A flush spreads across my skin. "Like me taking you like this, filling you up, fucking this drenched cunt of yours."

"Yes," I gasp, words barely forming as he strikes that sweet spot inside me. "Don't stop."

To my dismay, he does just that, withdrawing completely. Before I can utter a protest, he shifts lower, his breath scorching against my sensitive flesh. "Beau, wha—" My question dissolves into a throaty cry when his tongue finds my core, exploring and teasing with devastating finesse.

"So fuckin' sweet," he murmurs against me. He spreads me wider. His tongue delves between my swollen lips, moving with deliberate strokes that turn my legs to jelly. He circles my clit, then drags his tongue up through my folds, prodding at my core before moving to my ass.

I bury my face in the sheets at the raw intensity. He grips my thighs, steadying me as they begin to tremble, threatening to buckle under me.

He pulls away again and I whimper.

"Turn over," he commands with a light slap on my right ass cheek.

I gasp, mock-glaring at him over my shoulder and relishing in the naughty smirk on his lips.

He climbs onto the bed beside me and leans against the headboard. His eyes blaze with desire as I crawl to him on all fours.

"Come here, baby," he groans, eagerly reaching for me.

I straddle him, positioning myself above his cock. A bead of precum drips from the tip and down his thick shaft. His hands guide my hips as I sink down slowly, taking him inch by delicious inch until he's fully sheathed inside me. I shift my hips, drawing him in even deeper. With a groan, his head falls against the headboard.

His hold on me tightens as I begin to move. I find my rhythm, rising and falling as his hands explore my body—cupping my breasts, thumbs circling my nipples, then sliding down. The rough pad of his thumb finds my clit, circling it in perfect sync with every drop of my pussy.

The walls of my core start to flutter around his length and I grind against him, pulling my orgasm to the surface in moments. I cry out, my body singing with release.

"That's it, baby. Fuckin' beautiful," he growls, his eyes locked on me as I ride him in sloppy, wet ecstasy.

I throw my head back. "Oh, god, Beau!"

I collapse over him, my walls still fluttering around him when he takes over. He thrusts upward to meet each shaky, downward fall of my core. Another orgasm builds and I brace against the headboard beside his head as he slams into me from below. He grunts with each drag of his cock.

I shatter a second time with his name on my lips, my body wrung tight and clenching around him in waves. His release follows and he comes buried deep inside me. Ropes of hot cum paint me from the inside. I tremble at the feeling.

His arms wrap around me, holding me close as our heartbeats gradually slow to normal. He presses a kiss to my temple and I smile against his skin as his hand makes lazy patterns on my back.

"Welcome home," I say softly.

His hand stills and I tilt my head to face him. "You asking or telling?"

A small giggle slips out when he grins.

"Move in with me," I say, lifting up on an elbow to be face to face with him. I take in the stoic features I've grown to love so deeply. The strong jaw covered in stubble, the deep, dark eyes that see right through me, the stern mouth that can shift from commanding to tender in an instant—but only with me. "Officially. I mean, you've been staying here for the last month, living out of a duffle bag."

He hums. "True."

"And I love you," I tell him with a bat of my lashes and pout of my lips. Using my 'feminine wiles' against him, as he would say.

And boy, do they work.

"I love you, too." He tucks a strand of hair behind my ear. "Always will."

We lie tangled together for a few more minutes, savoring the quiet intimacy that feels like such a greater luxury than anything in Hollywood. After the premiere, we went to the afterparty for all of ten minutes—sneaking out the back to the hotel room.

The premiere feels like a distant dream: the cameras, the crowds, the critics. Reviews for the finale of *The Devil's Lake* trilogy have been overwhelmingly positive. It's made my little creative heart proud to see it gain so much love. And with shooting for my next project scheduled to begin in six months, Beau and I have *a lot* of decisions to make.

Reluctantly, Beau glances at his phone on the nightstand. "We should get moving," he says. "Cassidy asked if we could be there a few hours early for pictures. The wedding is at five, and we should feed Hulk beforehand."

At the mention of his name, Hulk lifts his head from his spot on the floor beside the bed, tail thumping against the hardwoods. His leg has healed remarkably well, barely a limp remaining. He was *ecstatic* to see us when we got home—*yes, even Beau*—although he certainly seemed reluctant to leave his new favorite little human.

Maci pulled me aside just the other day to ask if I would help them train the new puppy when he comes home in a few weeks. A blue heeler, Duke's dream dog. Which reportedly had him in tears when they got to meet the newest member of their family a few days ago.

Of course, I agreed.

I press one more kiss to Beau's cheek before I slide from the bed and head to the shower. My ass sways as I walk. A low groan followed by the bed creaking has me glancing over my shoulder at his hungry stare. When he moves to stand, gaze locked on mine, I scurry through the bathroom door and laugh as I close it quickly behind me.

✺

The Winton Resort sits nestled against the mountains like something out of a fairy tale. Sunlight glints off the glass of the main lodge, and wildflowers dot the surrounding meadows in splashes of purple, yellow, and white. The late June air carries the scent of pine and fresh mountain water, a welcome change from the stifling perfume of Hollywood.

"Wow," I breathe as Beau pulls the truck into the parking area. In all the months I've spent in Whitetail, not once have I come to the resort. Maci's invited me to several of her yoga classes, but I was too worried about the exposure, the tourists. I regret that decision. "This is gorgeous."

"Butch and Duke didn't spare any expense," Beau says, finding a spot between two lifted trucks. "Probably helped that they split the cost of everything."

I smile, remembering how Beau explained the unique wedding arrangement. His brothers had decided a year ago to share their special day—a double wedding that somehow makes perfect sense for the close-knit brothers.

"Ready?" Beau asks, cutting the engine. He looks handsome in his black suit and purple tie to match my flowy, purple floral dress that stops mid-calf. He was a good sport taking a butt load of pictures of me to send to Shea at her request.

"Absolutely." I've never been to a double wedding before. So much love, friends, family. It's exciting. And they were sweet enough to give Hulk his own invitation since Cassidy's dog, Frankie, is in attendance as well.

We're barely out of the truck with Hulk in tow, wearing a purple bowtie, when a familiar voice calls out. Duke's jogging toward us in a flawless black suit and tie, his usually composed face flushed with excitement or nerves. Probably both. "Thank god you're here," he says, clapping his brother on the shoulder before nodding a quick greeting to me. "Butch is driving everyone insane with last-minute checks, and Parker disappeared with the rings."

"He lost them already?" Beau asks, eyebrows raised.

"Not lost," Duke clarifies. "Just 'keeping them safe somewhere special' that he now can't remember."

I laugh as Beau huffs. "Where do you need me?"

"Groom's suite. Second floor of the lodge, east wing." Duke glances at his watch. "First look pictures are soon."

Beau turns to me. "You okay for a bit? I shouldn't be long."

"Go," I tell him with a smile. "I'll find a good seat for the ceremony."

He presses a quick kiss to my forehead before following Duke toward the lodge entrance. He falls into step with his brother. Hulk and I slowly make our way in the same direction.

The lodge interior is all polished wood and stone, with soaring ceilings and floor-to-ceiling windows that frame the mountain views. I follow signs toward the ceremony space, a stunning mountainside pavilion decorated with wildflowers and flowing white fabric. A few early guests are already being seated, people I recognize from around town.

I take a seat near the front on the far end so Hulk can lie down and place my purse on the chair next to me. It's not long before nearly every seat is full and a flurry of activity near the lodge draws everyone's attention. Two photographers are positioning themselves, and staff members are making final adjustments to the floral arrangements flanking the aisle.

I spot Beau a moment later, scanning the growing crowd, as ruggedly handsome as ever. When his eyes find me, his face relaxes into a smile that makes my heart skip. He makes his way over, greeting family members as he passes.

"Sorry about that," he says, sliding into the seat beside me. "Crisis averted. Rhett found the rings in the inside pocket of his jacket. Levi put them there, not Parker."

"Sounds stressful," I tease.

He shrugs. "Both of them are a mess, but trying hard to hide it." His arm settles around my chair, warm and solid. His hand brushes my arm. "You look beautiful."

A quiet 'aww' echoes around us and I blush despite myself.

Beau doesn't seem bothered by the audience, though, his focus remains on mine with an intensity that makes me forget the bustling activity around us. I smooth the skirt of my dress. "So do you."

Music begins to play, signaling guests to take their seats. Beau's hand finds mine as the music shifts to announce the start of the ceremony. I watch his face as the wedding party begins their procession—the subtle pride as Butch takes his place at the altar beside their uncle who is performing the ceremony and as his and Cassidy's bridesmaids and groomsmen pair off down the aisle. When Cassidy appears at the entrance in a stunning ball gown with a man I recognize on her arm and a chubby wiener dog trotting in front of her, my eyes go wide.

I nudge Beau with my elbow. "Oh, my *god*. Is that...Garrett Clark?" The hottest country-rock singer to hit the radio in the last decade. Shea would *die* if she were here. She's obsessed with his song *Whiskey Bent*. Heck, I think we all are.

"Yeah, that's Cassidy's brother," he confirms. "Butch helped him get sober a few years ago. Don't think he's been back to town since. Supposedly, he met some guy in rehab who helped him get his song out."

As the ceremony unfolds, I find myself watching Beau almost as much as the proceedings. Butch and Cassidy have their ceremony first; Duke stands beside him as his best man while Maci watches from the far back row so not to draw attention away from their special moment. The gloss in Butch's eyes when he recites his vows to Cassidy has everyone in tears. They kiss and applause follows them down the aisle where they stand at the back of the crowd. Duke takes Butch's place at the altar.

A new song plays, and Maci glides to him in an elegant satin gown. Their moment is just as beautiful. Duke stumbles in his promise to Maci, but she beams, brushing a stray tear from his cheek.

I sniffle and Beau squeezes my hand. I glance at him. His rapt attention is on his family. The love he has for his brothers is written plainly across his face, unguarded in a way he rarely allows himself to be.

When the final couple is pronounced husband and wife, the pavilion erupts in cheers and applause, and something flashes across his expression—a brief, considering look as his gaze meets mine that makes my breath catch.

The recessional music swells as the newlyweds make their way back down the aisle, followed by the wedding party. Guests begin to stir, gathering purses and suit jackets as they prepare to move to the reception area.

"That was beautiful," I say, blinking back tears.

Beau's thumb brushes across my cheek, catching a stray drop I didn't realize had fallen. "It was," he agrees, his gaze never leaving mine.

There's a weight to his gaze that makes me wonder what he's thinking, but before I can ask, we're swept up in the crowd. His hand remains firmly in mine as we navigate through family and friends.

The evening sun casts long shadows across the resort grounds as we follow the flow of guests toward the reception tent. In the distance, the newlyweds are posing for photos against the mountain backdrop, their joy visible even from afar.

"Do you need to join them?" I ask, nodding toward where his parents stand with the wedding party.

Beau shakes his head. "Not yet. Family photos are after the cocktail hour." His arm slides around my waist, drawing me closer. "Which means I get you all to myself for a little while."

"Whatever will we do with this time?" I ask innocently.

His grin turns mischievous. "I have a few ideas."

Twenty-Seven.

Callie

THE RECEPTION IS IN full swing by the time the speeches conclude. The dance floor is crowded with guests moving to the live band's upbeat cover of a country song, the overhead string lights cast a warm glow over the celebration.

I sit at our table, while Beau chats with a cousin near the bar. Even from across the tent, I can see the relaxed set of his shoulders, the easy smile that appears more frequently now than when we first met. He looks at home here.

"He hasn't taken his eyes off you all night, you know." Julie, Beau's mom, slides into the chair beside me. She's elegantly dressed in a navy jumpsuit with flowy sleeves, her silver-blonde hair swept into a stylish updo. "Even when he's talking to someone else, he checks to make sure you're okay. He's quite fond of you."

Warmth rises to my cheeks. "He's protective."

"It's more than that, dear." She pats my hand, her eyes kind but knowing. "He's always been the serious one, the careful one. Even before the army."

I nod, recognizing the description of the man I first met—guarded, watchful, keeping the world at arm's length.

"But the way he looks at you?" Julie continues. "That's new. That's a man who's found his place."

The band transitions to a slower song, and as if summoned by our conversation, Beau appears before us, hand extended toward me. "Dance with me?" he asks deeply, merely sparing his mother a sweeping glance.

I place my hand in his and tell Hulk to stay. He sits beside Julie watching on with a satisfied smile, as Beau leads me to the dance floor. His arm circles my waist, drawing me close as we begin to sway to the music.

"Having fun?" he asks, his voice low near my ear.

"Yes," I answer honestly. "Your family is wonderful."

"She likes you," he says, glancing at our table.

I roll my eyes. "What, did she tell you that?"

"She did." His smirk is slow, easy. "They all did."

His hand is warm against the small of my back, one I've come to rely on. We move together easily, finding our rhythm among the other couples on the dance floor. Duke and Maci glide past us, lost in their own world. Nearby, Butch twirls Cassidy in a move that fumbles but makes her laugh.

"Do you ever think about it?" I ask, the question slipping out before I can reconsider.

"About what?"

I nod subtly to the newlyweds. "Marriage."

Beau tightens his hold on my waist. Fingers flexing in thought. "After everything...it didn't seem like it was in the cards for me."

I peer at him. My hopeful heart in my throat when I ask, "And now?"

His gaze finds mine, deep and serious. "I think about a lot of things I didn't before."

My heart beats faster. We haven't been together long—a few months—but there's a certainty to what we've built. I can't see myself with anyone else. "Like what?" I press gently.

A smile curves his lips. "Like putting an addition on your cabin or making the new one bigger. Adding a matching porch swing to the back porch so we can watch the sunset every night. Or how I wake up early just to see the sunrise reflect in your eyes when you first wake up."

My breath catches. "Those are very specific thoughts."

"I'm a specific kind of man." His hand tightens on mine. "I don't do anything these days without thinking of you, sweetheart."

The implication hangs between us. Heartfelt and so much more. Before I can respond, the song ends, and the band announces it's time for the cake cutting. Beau leads me off the dance floor, my hand firmly in his.

As the couples take turns feeding each other cake—with Butch predictably smearing frosting on Cassidy's nose to the delight of the crowd—Beau's arm slips around my waist again.

"For the record," he murmurs against my hair, my back pressed to his front, "when I do ask you, it'll be because I can't go another day without knowing you're mine completely."

The simple *when*, not *if*, sends a shiver through me. I lean into him, overwhelmed by the rush of emotions. "You have me now," I say softly, peering at him.

He hums as he tilts my chin. He kisses me sweetly. "I do."

The evening progresses with more dancing, more champagne, more laughter. I find myself drawn into conversations with various Montgomery relatives, each with their own stories about Beau growing up. His brother, Levi, shows me photos of teenage Beau with a retainer and an unfortunate haircut, while Uncle Jim recounts how Beau once built an entire treehouse by himself at age twelve. "It was a simple platform," he tells me, "but he was so damn proud of himself." I hang on every word, every detail about Beau I can. And love each one.

The band shifts to slower, mellower songs, and the energy of the reception transforms into something more intimate. Beau and I share another dance as guests begin to leave. I yawn a few times and we decide to call it a night.

"I need to grab my purse from the table quick," I tell him when the song ends.

"I'll get it," he offers. "Meet you by the entrance?"

I nod, patting my leg for Hulk to follow. The night air is cool after the warmth of the crowded reception, and I take a moment to appreciate the stars visible above the mountain peaks.

Movement near the side entrance of the main lodge catches my eye. An employee or utility entrance, I think? A woman emerges, adjusting her dress as she glances around. Even in the dim lighting, I recognize Lily, Beau's sister. Her hair mussed, lipstick smudged at one corner.

She doesn't notice me standing in the shadows a mere ten feet away as she quickly smooths her hair and heads back toward the reception. I fight back a rude giggle. Secret public sex at your brother's wedding? I didn't peg Lily for that kind of thing.

Completely unable to stop my curiosity from killing me, I remain where I am, wondering who is on the other side of that door. I don't have to wait long. The same door opens again, and a tall figure steps out, tucking his shirt back into his pants.

I slap a hand over my mouth to contain my shock. Garrett Clark.

Holy—

He hasn't seen me yet, his attention focused on straightening his tie and checking his reflection in a darkened window. I step deeper into the shadows, tugging Hulk back with me a step. I don't know why I'm hiding, though it's probably instinct telling me I just saw something I wasn't meant to see.

They'd been seated at different tables, showing no particular interest in each other all night. At least, none that I'd noticed. Clearly, there was more happening than wedding small talk.

Beau calls my name, approaching with my purse in hand, his face curious at finding me lurking in the darkness. "Everything okay?" he asks.

I glance to where Garrett was standing, but he's gone. "Yeah," I say, taking my purse. "Just...enjoying the view."

Beau's gaze searches mine. "Bullshit."

I snort-laugh. "I'll tell you later. Promise."

He nods, accepting my answer while offering me his arm as we walk to the truck. Hulk is curled up in the backseat, exhausted from a day of being fawned over by wedding guests. The drive is peaceful, the Montana night sky stretching endlessly above us, stars brilliant and bright. I roll down my window, letting the cool mountain air wash over me.

Six months ago, I fled to this place in hopes of finding solitude and safety. A means to an end. Instead, I found a grumpy landlord who became so much more.

"What are you thinking about?" he asks as we turn onto the familiar road leading to the cabin. "You've got that look."

"What look?"

"The one where you're turning something over and over in your mind." He glances at me before returning his focus to the road.

I smile at how well he knows me already. "Just thinking about us."

He reaches across the console to take my hand, his thumb brushing across my knuckles like a silent declaration. I squeeze his hand in response. *I love you, too.*

When we arrive at the cabin, he unlocks the door, holding it open for Hulk and me. I step into the space that has become more home to me than any place I've ever lived. Beau moves behind me, his hands settling on my shoulders to massage away the tension from hours of mingling and dancing.

His arms encircle me, holding me close as his lips find my temple. "Being here with you," he murmurs, "it's more than I ever thought I'd have. More than I thought I deserved."

I turn in his arms, gazing at the face I've come to crave the sight of every morning. I smile softly. "And what do you think you deserve now?"

His gaze holds mine with an intense certainty I can't explain.

The love I feel from this man is...

"Everything," he says. "With you."

The word echoes between us. *Everything*. I rise on tiptoes to kiss him, knowing I want the same thing.

Everything. With him.

For the first time in years, I'm not hiding from my future.

I'm living for it.

And it feels like finally coming home.

Epilogue.

Beau

Two months later...

I FUMBLE WITH TYING the ring box to Hulk's collar. He huffs as my shaky hands drop the velvet black box for a third time. "Shit," I hiss.

Hulk gives me a look that can only be described as judgmental.

"Don't start with me," I grunt, retrieving the box from the cabin floor.

His tail thumps once against the hardwood, unimpressed with my nerves. I can't blame him. I've faced insurgents with steadier hands than these. Outside, Callie's moving around on the back porch, arranging the blankets and mugs she brought out for our evening ritual. Watching the sunset has become our thing over the past five months—a quiet moment at the end of each day to just be together.

Tonight, if I can get this damn box secured, it'll mean far more going forward.

I finally manage to loop the ribbon through Hulk's collar, knotting it with what I hope is enough security to keep the ring in place until the right moment. I adjust the box, making sure it's visible but not uncomfortable for him.

"Remember the plan," I tell him seriously. "When I call you over, bring this to Callie. That's it. Simple."

Hulk tilts his head.

"There'll be a steak in it for you," I add, resorting to bribery.

That gets his attention. His ears perk up, and I *swear* he nods in agreement.

"Good boy." I scratch behind his ears, then take a deep breath. "Let's do this."

I lead Hulk through the living room toward the back door, careful to keep him on my far side so Callie won't immediately spot the box. My heart hammers against my ribs with each step. It's ridiculous, really. I know she loves me. We've been inseparable for months now. The ring feels like a formality at this point.

So why the hell are my palms sweating as I step onto the porch?

She looks up from where she's arranging a throw blanket on the swing, and the sight of her still hits me like the first time. Her hair is loose around her shoulders, catching the golden light of the setting sun. She's wearing one of my flannel shirts over leggings, the sleeves rolled up to her elbows. Nothing fancy. No elegant ball gown. Just...Callie. My girl. Comfortable and at home.

"There you are," she says with a smile. "I was beginning to think you'd gotten lost in there."

I grunt, not knowing how to respond. I guide Hulk to sit beside the swing. The box dangles from his collar, and I position myself to block Callie's view of it. She passes me a mug of Earl Grey, the steam rising between us.

"Everything okay?" she asks, sipping her tea. "You seem tense."

"Never better," I assure her, sitting beside her on the swing. I sip from the mug, barely tasting it through my nerves. She settles against me and I put my arm around her shoulders.

I take a deep breath of cool, September air as the sunset spreads before us, painting the mountains in shades of purple and gold. Our cleared land stretches toward the tree line, evidence of the work we've put into making this place ours. The garden she insisted on planting is still producing late summer vegetables. The new shed I built stands completed to the right, housing my tools and her outdoor writing space.

"It's so beautiful tonight," she murmurs, watching the colors shift across the sky.

"Yeah," I agree, though my gaze is trained on her, not the sunset.

We sit in comfortable silence for a few minutes, the swing creaking gently beneath us. I'm waiting for the perfect moment, when the sun hits the peaks, and the words I've rehearsed a hundred times will finally come out.

"Oh," Callie says suddenly, spotting something near our feet. "What'd you find, Hulk?"

I glance down to see the box on the porch floor, the ribbon having slipped free from his collar. Before I can react, Hulk picks it up in his mouth and drops it directly into Callie's lap, looking entirely too pleased with himself.

So much for that planned moment.

Callie stares down at the signature velvet box, then at me, her eyes widening with realization. "Beau?" Her voice is soft, questioning.

I take a deep breath. No going back now.

I set my mug aside and take the box from her lap, shifting off the swing to face her as I drop to one knee—the stunning Montana sunset now at my back. Her little gasp has me sweating and grinning and eager to get this right. "Callie—"

"Yes!" she blurts with a squeal, her feet hopping without touching the ground.

"Will you—"

"Oh my gosh, yes."

I throw my head back on a chuckle.

She hides her face, tears in her eyes even as her cheeks pinken. "I'm so sorry, I just..."

"I love you, too, sweetheart."

Her wobbly smile and teary eyes are all I need. My girl doesn't need the big speech, the fancy lifestyle. She makes me feel like I'm the only damn thing she'll ever need.

"You're it, sweetheart," I say. "I don't want to spend another day without you by my side. I want everything with you," I tell her, echoing the words that have become our promise to each other. "Every sunrise, every sunset, every moment in between." I open the ring box in my hand, revealing a pear-shaped diamond on a diamond-studded band—chosen with the help of Shea.

"Will you marry me?"

She throws herself at me and we're a mixture of tears and laughter. Her lips land on mine. "I love you," she whispers against me.

I chuckle. "Is that a yes?"

"Yes," she says against my lips. "Yes, of course, I'll marry you."

I kiss her then, tasting salt from her tears and sweetness that's distinctly hers. When we finally part, I take her hand, sliding the ring onto her finger with steady hands.

"It's perfect," she whispers, looking at the ring, then at me. "You're perfect."

"Far from it," I say with a laugh. "But I'm yours."

"Mine," she agrees, taking my face in her hands and kissing me again. "And I'm yours."

The End.

Thanks for reading!
Please leave a review to let me know what you thought.

Ready for more Montgomery brothers? Keep reading for a sneak
peak of Rhett's story in Book Four: Restored by You.

XO,
A. Boss

Restored by You

Rhett

THE SLAM OF THE front door tells me two things: Levi is home and he's in a sour mood.

I focus on the bacon sizzling in the pan in front of me. "Hungry?" I call out, flipping the bacon and hissing when the grease pops, landing on my wrist. I swipe it away and drop the lid over the pan with a *clang*.

"Have you seen this shit?" my brother hollers from down the hall, grumbling something under his breath about the family group chat I set up at Ma's request a few months ago when Beau returned home. It's usually pictures of the grandkids, updates on

Sunday dinner attendance, or weather-related, but every now and then, big news drops in the ol' Montgomery text chain.

The side chats are where the *real* family drama lies.

"Yep," I say, knowing he's referring to the engagement announcement Beau shared—his second message ever sent in the chat. His first was, *Who is this?*

Beau told me a few weeks ago about his plan to propose to Callie when he used 'helping Rhett' as an excuse for why he was gone half the day. In reality, he was picking up the custom ring from a jewelry shop in Billings.

Levi comes around the corner from the living room, appearing in the archway connecting to the open concept kitchen we just finished last spring. He tosses his hoodie over the back of the couch and plops onto a bar stool at the end of the island.

His blond hair flops and he sighs, "I'm going to die alone."

If it's not one brother, it's another.

I roll my eyes and return them to the stovetop. "Relax."

"How can I relax? Brit won't answer my calls."

My jaw tightens and I spin a glare on my beloved, yet moronic, brother. "She's going to put a restraining order on your ass if you don't dial it back."

He huffs dramatically. "You can't restrain love, Rhett."

"She's not the one, man." I shake my head, asking, "BLT?" I transfer the bacon onto a paper plate and set the pan to the side, turning off the stove before heading for the fridge.

"Sure," he says, rising to grab the bread from the far counter.

I return with the lettuce and sliced tomato leftover from yesterday's lunch. I even grab a few slices of cheese for Levi—knowing he's sad and prefers a BLT *with* cheese, making it more of a BLT+C.

He's a strange one when it comes to his dairy products.

"How the hell are you okay with all of this?"

I raise a brow and glance at him. "With what?"

"Butch, Duke." He ticks off a finger with each name. "And now *Beau*. Fuckin' Beau is getting hitched before me, or you. It's bullshit."

I shrug a shoulder and slide his plate to him, then pick up my sandwich and take an oversized bite. It's after ten o'clock at night and this is the second thing I've eaten all day. Work has been crazy with everyone trying to fit in last-minute renovations before the trifecta of the holiday season hits.

"It is what it is," I mumble around a mouthful.

He takes his plate to the island and sits. "I hate that saying."

I do, too, but it's the truth.

I swallow and grab two longnecks from the fridge. I pop the tops and hand one to my brother. We drink and eat in silence, neither of us wanting to dive into all the reasons why we're single, why I've stopped dating altogether, and why Levi can't seem to stop searching for his elusive *The One*.

We finish eating, and the second I start to clean up, Levi is making himself scarce. "Thanks for dinner," he says and promptly yawns. "What time do you need me to meet you at the resort tomorrow?"

The urge to tell him not to bother is on the tip of my tongue. I love my brother to death, probably more than the rest of 'em, but sometimes...his priorities aren't in line with the growing company we've had since we were sixteen: *Montgomery Construction & Lumber.*

Too young to know what the hell we were getting into, and too dumb to realize how smart we were for doing it.

"Eleven. And don't be late. This is a huge opportunity for us. It'll look good for both owners to be there." I've always handled the bulk of the business—the quotes, the scheduling, the books, the accounts—while Levi shows up where he's needed.

The guy can do it all with his eyes closed as far as construction is concerned, and he's one hell of a carpenter. But if you ask him his password to his bank account, or where he parked his truck when coming out of the grocery store, he'll stare at you like you have three heads.

We've lived together our whole lives; we know each other well enough to acknowledge our strengths and weaknesses. When to push and when not to. I don't hold any of them against him.

Although, his desperate *need* to find love is getting out of hand these last few months.

"You got it." He stretches and heads for the stairs. "Night, bro."

"Night," I say, scraping the grease off the pan into the trash before washing it.

I'm just turning off the lights to head up when my phone vibrates in my pocket. I groan, "Fuck." Fishing it out, I glance at the name on the screen. Brow furrowed, I answer. "Hello?"

"Hey, Rhett," Callie rushes out on the other end. "I'm so sorry to be calling you this late, but it's an emergency."

I straighten and head for the door. "What's going on? You guys all right?" I tug on my boots, bending to stuff the laces in the sides before grabbing my keys off the hook.

"We're fine," Beau grunts, revealing I'm on speakerphone.

I pause, hand on the doorknob.

"Everyone is fine," his fiancée says. "Sorry, I probably should have led with that."

"What—"

"My friend, Shea. She just bought a fixer-upper in town; it's right down the road from you," she tells me. "And she, um, well, I'm not sure *what* the heck she did, but now there's water running down the stairs. We think it might be a pipe or the bathroom or—I have no idea; I'm not a plumber."

I tilt the phone away from my face and take a deep breath. *Neither am I*, I want to argue, but instead—being the brother always on call—I say, "What's the address?"

Get ready for the next Montgomery looking for love in
Restored by You,
Book Four: Montgomery Brothers of Montana!

Sign up for my newsletter at abossauthor.com and receive the FREE, insta-love story of Clayton & Julie, prequel novella to Montgomery Brothers of Montana!

Note from the Author

Thank you for choosing to pick up this book and read it! It means so much to me that you chose to spend your time reading something that I wrote. If I could hug you through this page, I would.

I hope you loved this enough to come back for more, because I certainly intend to put more out in the world from the *Boss Babe Universe*!

Don't forget to sign-up for my newsletter <u>HERE</u> and receive your *FREE* copy of *Only by You*, the insta-love story of Clayton & Julie, prequel novella to Montgomery Brothers of Montana!

Are you a *Boss Babe*?

Join the *Boss Babe Universe* on Facebook, Twitter/X, and Instagram!

About the Author

A. Boss writes steamy, contemporary romance featuring grumpy heroes, protective alphas, and sassy heroines. Her books promise sweet and sexy banter, small-town gossip that keeps you turning pages, and swoony happily ever afters that will leave you breathless.

She lives in upstate New York with her husband, two crazy kids, and two sleepy dachshunds who are definitely the real bosses.

Perfect for readers who crave steamy, heartfelt romance with all the feels and happily ever afters guaranteed.

You can follow her on all the social media platforms for updates, freebies, and sneak peeks at upcoming releases. Twitter/X, Facebook, Instagram – whatever your poison may be – drop by and say hello!

Everyone is welcome in the *Boss Babe Universe*!

Acknowledgements

A huge thank you to my critique ladies, beta readers, and dare I say it...*fans* of the Montgomery Brothers series! Sarah (sorry not sorry about the weeping cocks, LOL), Colleen, Jill, and Sevannah – I appreciate all of you!

Also, shout out to the first book I ever wrote that was mentioned in *this* book: *The Devil's Lake.*

Will you ever see the light of day? That remains to be seen...